SPAWN®: ESCALATION
ISBN 1 85286 831 7

Published by Titan Books Ltd
42 - 44 Dolben St
London SE1 0UP
In association with Image Comics™

This book collects issues 16 – 20 of the Image Comics' series *Spawn*.
Also collected in the USA as *Spawn Volume 4*.

British Library Cataloguing-In-Publication data. A catalogue record for this
book is available from the British Library.

First edition: August 1997
10 9 8 7 6 5 4 3 2 1

Printed in Italy.

T I T A N   B O O K S
in association with IMAGE COMICS™

Hellspawn. The Devil's own. Officers-in-training in the army of Hell. Juicy, choice souls, shaped and honed by arch-demon Malebolgia for the time when all Hell will rise up and storm the gates of Heaven itself. Pulled by his own needs into a bargain of infernal proportions, Al Simmons traded his soul without thought for the consequences, even though every fibre of his being screamed "no!". Now he is lost. Damned. And all for nought. This is Spawn's lot, his destiny.

Al Simmons had been a soldier in the past, before he was murdered and recreated as Spawn, fighting wars that the general public never even knew existed, living life in a shadow realm of infiltration, destabilisation and assassination. All for his country, never questioning or counting the cumulative cost to his immortal soul. Al Simmons followed orders to the end, and was betrayed and killed by his own without qualm or remorse.

So much lost. His life, much of his memory, and — most unbearably, as it was for her he came back, for her he traded his soul — his wife Wanda Blake. Remarried to his best friend and former co-worker Terry Fitzgerald and now mother to five year-old Cyan, Wanda is just another part of his lost past, a living testament to a happiness now forever denied him.

Malebolgia lied, cheated, deceived, but in the end Al Simmons has only himself to blame. He was lost long before Malebolgia made his empty promises, long before even Chapel pulled the trigger that ended his life.

Chapel. A man he worked with, fought with. A

man he trusted with his life, and who betrayed that trust at point-blank range, consigning him to the fiery clutches of Hell. At last he knows. Who pulled the trigger. Who killed Al Simmons. Finally, after confused weeks stumbling blindly in a mist of ethereal memories and half-truths, he knows.

But the knowledge, and the savage revenge that follows, bring no peace. Gathering thunderheads, brooding harbingers of further turmoil and chaos, darken still further, rolling in ominous harmony with Spawn's own storm-tossed thoughts.

Around him, stalking, closing in... demons, angels, dark-suited 'spooks', zealous cops and vengeful hoods. All of them, wanting a piece of Spawn.

Out there somewhere, trapped in its grotesquely comical Clown persona, the Violator; a predatory insectile demon of lethal power. Trapped. But for how long? The memory of their initial battle is keen, the wounds still deep and barely healed. Would he survive a second encounter, Spawn wonders? His own power is finite, a well sunk only a short distance into the hellish subterranean source that feeds it. He's died once, he doesn't relish the experience a second time.

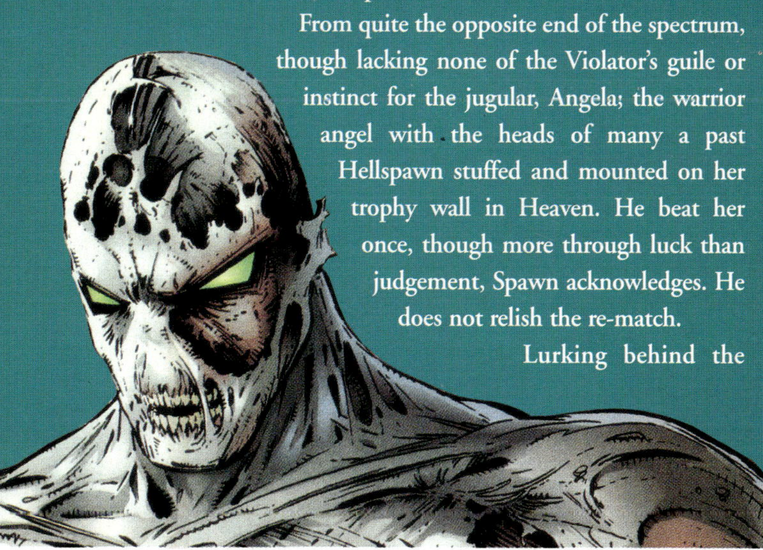

From quite the opposite end of the spectrum, though lacking none of the Violator's guile or instinct for the jugular, Angela; the warrior angel with the heads of many a past Hellspawn stuffed and mounted on her trophy wall in Heaven. He beat her once, though more through luck than judgement, Spawn acknowledges. He does not relish the re-match.

Lurking behind the

scenes, pulling strings and subtly guiding events, his former boss Jason Wynn. Chapel may have pulled the trigger, but who gave the order? How long before Wynn realises, Spawn muses, that the job was only part done? If nothing else, Wynn has a habit of not leaving loose ends, especially ones with knowledge of his shadowy dealings.

And Tony Twist, the mob boss who believes Spawn to be responsible for a swathe cut through his ranks by the Violator. And Overt-Kill, the deranged cyborg murder machine hired by Twist to kill Spawn.

And NYPD detectives Sam Burke and 'Twitch' Williams, searching for the costumed vigilante known as Spawn.

And... And... And...

This is Spawn's lot, his destiny. Denied his wife and the love that sustained him, cast out from the life he once led, hounded and attacked again and again and again. This is Spawn's lot, his destiny. But he's not going to take it lying down!

SPAWN
image
DEC
16
$1.95
$2.46 Canada
TM

E F L E C T I O N S
Part one

"THERE IT IS, MAJOR VALE. THAT'S THE PLACE.
"I CALL IT SIMMONSVILLE. PRIVATE JOKE.
"'VOLUNTEERS.'
"WE'RE QUITE SAFE HERE, OF COURSE, BUT I'D LIKE YOU TO KEEP A CLOSE WATCH ON OUR TWO... WELL, WHAT CAN I CALL THEM? NOT GUINEA PIGS.
JEEZ, HOW'D WE GET OURSELVES INTO THIS ONE, BREWER? THIS PLACE IS FREAKIN' ME OUT TOTALLY, MAN.
YOU EVER BEEN TO DISNEYLAND?
SURE I'VE BEEN TO DISNEYLAND. WHAT THE HELL'S THAT GOT TO DO WITH ANYTHING?
I DUNNO, IT JUST KINDA REMINDS ME OF THIS PLACE.
IT'S LIKE NOTHING FITS, YOU KNOW? THERE'S A CHURCH RIGHT NEXT TO A WATER-SLIDE AND A FACTORY IN THE MIDDLE OF A PARK AND THE WHOLE PLACE IS DESERTED LIKE IT...
HEADS UP, STEVENS! WE GOT INCOMING!
KRRAAATCH
"WELCOME TO SIMMONSVILLE, MAJOR VALE.

"OUR VERY OWN LITTLE PIECE OF HELL ON EARTH."

oh my
God

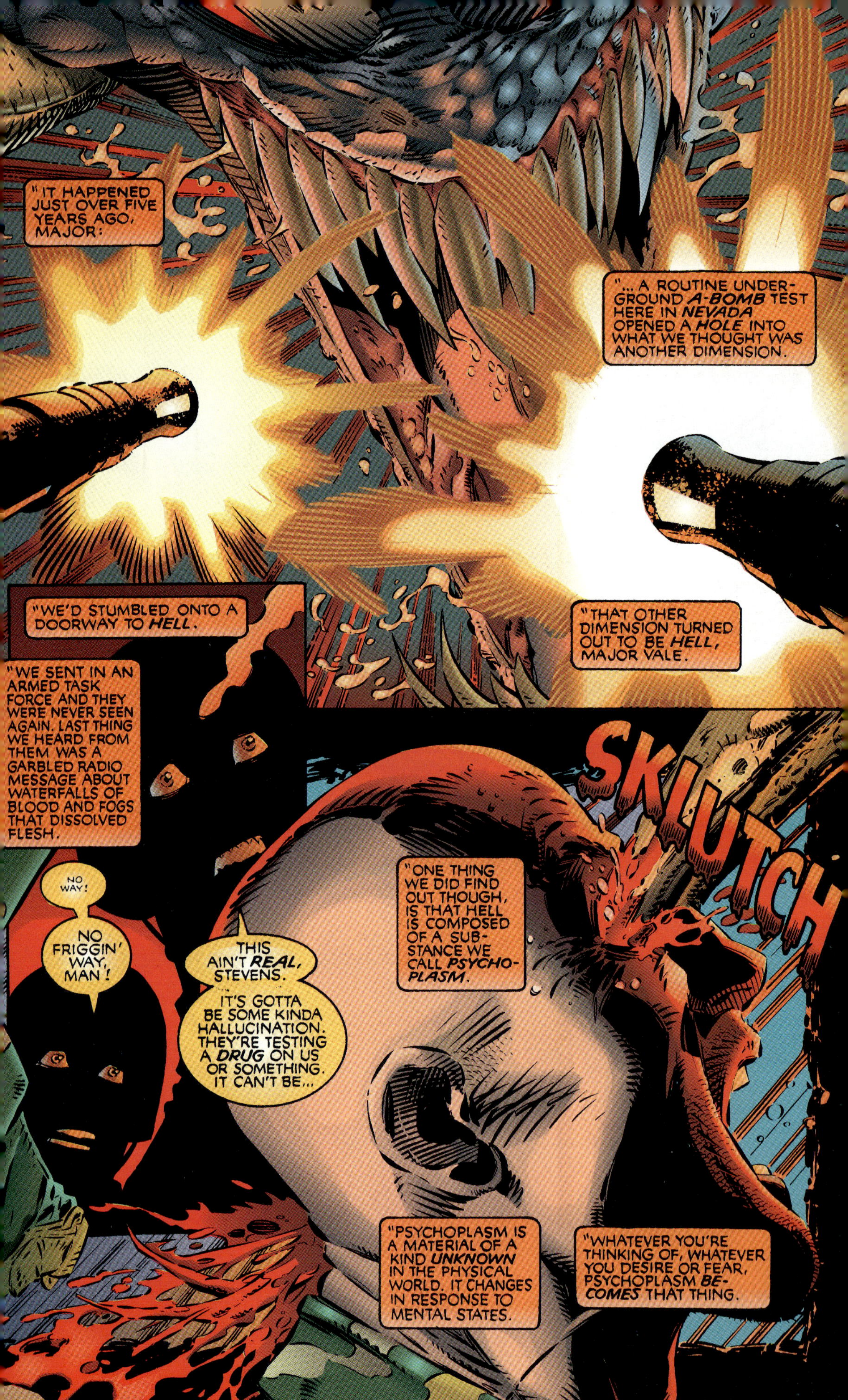

"IT HAPPENED JUST OVER FIVE YEARS AGO, MAJOR:
"... A ROUTINE UNDER-GROUND A-BOMB TEST HERE IN NEVADA OPENED A HOLE INTO WHAT WE THOUGHT WAS ANOTHER DIMENSION.
"WE'D STUMBLED ONTO A DOORWAY TO HELL.
"THAT OTHER DIMENSION TURNED OUT TO BE HELL, MAJOR VALE.
"WE SENT IN AN ARMED TASK FORCE AND THEY WERE NEVER SEEN AGAIN. LAST THING WE HEARD FROM THEM WAS A GARBLED RADIO MESSAGE ABOUT WATERFALLS OF BLOOD AND FOGS THAT DISSOLVED FLESH.
NO WAY!
NO FRIGGIN' WAY, MAN!
THIS AIN'T REAL, STEVENS.
IT'S GOTTA BE SOME KINDA HALLUCINATION. THEY'RE TESTING A DRUG ON US OR SOMETHING. IT CAN'T BE...
"ONE THING WE DID FIND OUT THOUGH, IS THAT HELL IS COMPOSED OF A SUB-STANCE WE CALL PSYCHO-PLASM.
SKLUTCH
"PSYCHOPLASM IS A MATERIAL OF A KIND UNKNOWN IN THE PHYSICAL WORLD. IT CHANGES IN RESPONSE TO MENTAL STATES.
"WHATEVER YOU'RE THINKING OF, WHATEVER YOU DESIRE OR FEAR, PSYCHOPLASM BE-COMES THAT THING.

WHERE ARE YOU, LARRY?
WHERE ARE YOU?
BRAKABRAKABRAK
BREWER!
Oh JESUS...
BOO!
YAAAA!
NOOOO
"JUST IMAGINE WHAT IT WOULD MEAN TO THE U.S. MILITARY IF WE COULD GAIN CONTROL OF SUCH A SUBSTANCE, MAJOR VALE.
"WHICH BRINGS ME TO AL SIMMONS.
BREWER?
LARRY?

DON'T HURT ME.
PLEASE DON'T... I GOT A WIFE... PLEASE...
"SIMMONS WAS A GOOD MAN, ONE OF OUR BEST. GOD KNOWS, I TRAINED HIM MYSELF, TAUGHT HIM EVERYTHING I KNOW. BUT HE WENT SOFT, HE BECAME EXPENDABLE AND SO I MADE A DEAL.
"THERE ARE... PRESENCES IN HELL, MAJOR. I CONTACTED ONE OF THOSE PRESENCES AND MADE A DEAL WITH IT. I GAVE IT SIMMONS FOR ITS ARMY, IT GAVE ME PSYCHOPLASM.
GIMME A BREAK, SOLDIER.
"THE TOWN YOU'RE LOOKING AT, THE TOWN WHERE OUR TWO UNFORTUNATE VOLUNTEERS ARE CURRENTLY FACING THEIR WORST NIGHTMARES, IS COMPOSED ENTIRELY OF PSYCHOPLASM.
WILL YA QUIT WITH THE 'GOD' ALLA TIME?
YER MAKIN' ME NAUSEOUS.
STOP! PLEASE!
oh GOD!
STOP!
SHOW SOME SPINE, WHY DON'CHA? YOUR BUDDY SURE DID. Hee hee.
BA DUMP
"WHEN WE SENT SIMMONS TO HELL, WE STOLE HIS MEMORIES. THOSE MEMORIES, ACTING UPON RAW PSYCHOPLASM, CREATED SIMMONSVILLE-- A FAKE TOWN BUILT FROM THE JUMBLE OF ONE MAN'S RECOLLECTIONS.
"HOUSES THAT HE LIVED IN, THE SCHOOLS HE WENT TO, PLAYGROUNDS HE PLAYED IN, FACTORIES AND CHURCHES AND PARKS-- ALL RECREATED HERE IN THE DESERT, ABOVE THE DOORWAY TO HELL.
NOOoo
BA DUMP

"THIS IS WHERE WE'VE BEEN CONDUCTING OUR RESEARCH, MAJOR. THIS IS WHAT I WANTED YOU TO SEE.
SLAM!
INTERESTED?
THAT'S THE CRAZIEST GODDAMN THING I EVER HEARD, MR. WYNN, BUT I CAN'T DENY WHAT I JUST SAW WITH MY OWN EYES.
THOSE THINGS WERE... DEMONS? IS THAT WHAT YOU'RE TELLIN' ME?
I JUST DON'T KNOW HOW I CAN TAKE THIS ON BOARD... I...
IT IS ALL A LITTLE OVERWHELMING, MAJOR VALE. I CAN UNDERSTAND THAT.
WHY NOT THINK THINGS OVER AND WE'LL TALK AGAIN IN AN HOUR OR TWO, WHEN I'VE COMPLETED MY DAILY WORKOUT.
HOW DOES THAT SOUND?

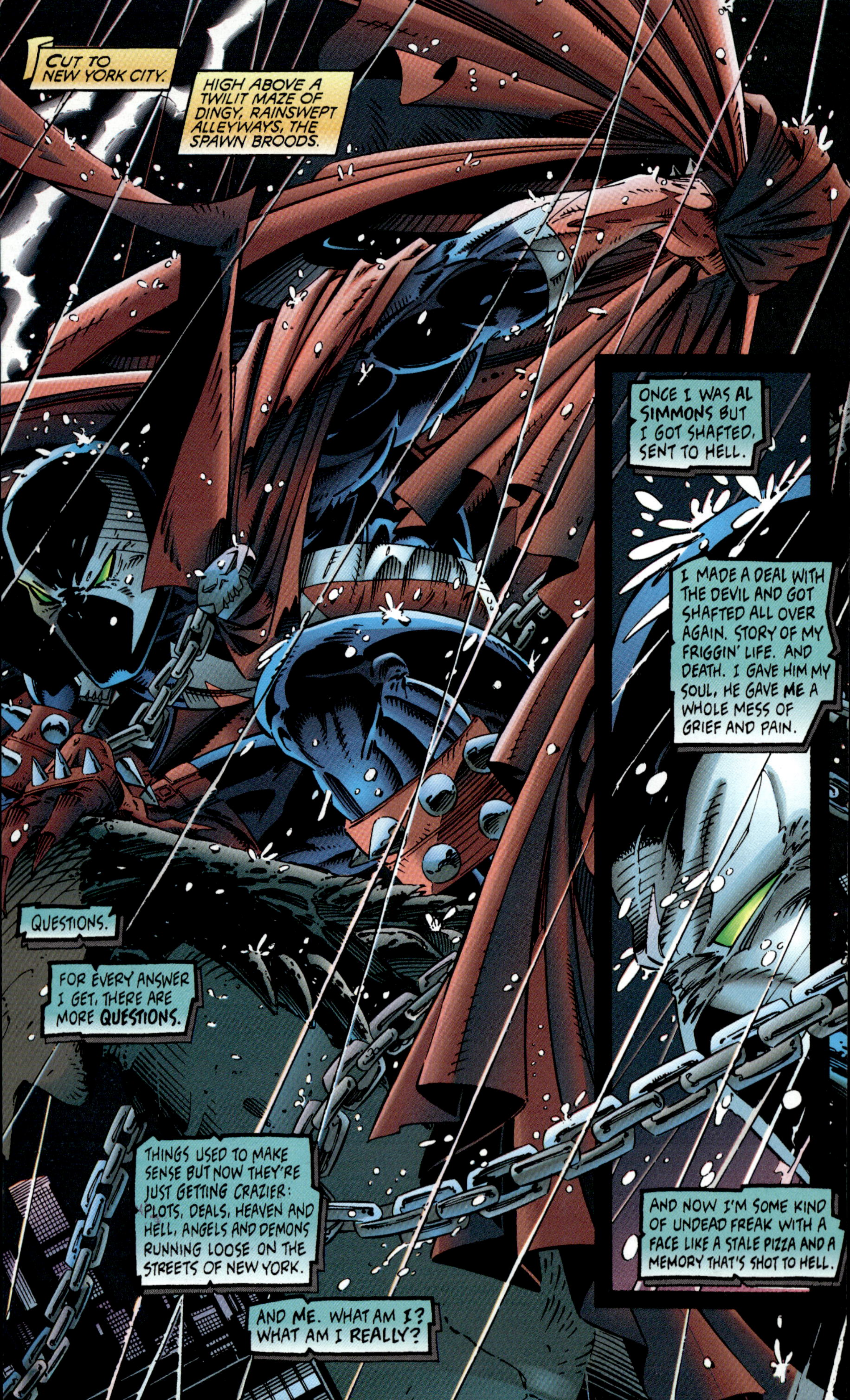

CUT TO NEW YORK CITY.

HIGH ABOVE A TWILIT MAZE OF DINGY, RAINSWEPT ALLEYWAYS, THE SPAWN BROODS.

ONCE I WAS AL SIMMONS BUT I GOT SHAFTED, SENT TO HELL.

I MADE A DEAL WITH THE DEVIL AND GOT SHAFTED ALL OVER AGAIN. STORY OF MY FRIGGIN' LIFE. AND DEATH. I GAVE HIM MY SOUL, HE GAVE ME A WHOLE MESS OF GRIEF AND PAIN.

QUESTIONS.

FOR EVERY ANSWER I GET, THERE ARE MORE QUESTIONS.

THINGS USED TO MAKE SENSE BUT NOW THEY'RE JUST GETTING CRAZIER: PLOTS, DEALS, HEAVEN AND HELL, ANGELS AND DEMONS RUNNING LOOSE ON THE STREETS OF NEW YORK.

AND NOW I'M SOME KIND OF UNDEAD FREAK WITH A FACE LIKE A STALE PIZZA AND A MEMORY THAT'S SHOT TO HELL.

AND ME. WHAT AM I? WHAT AM I REALLY?

I'M FINDING OUT MORE AND MORE EVERY DAY BUT I STILL DON'T KNOW WHAT REALLY HAPPENED OR WHAT I REALLY AM.
AL SIMMONS IS DEAD. CHAPEL PULLED THE TRIGGER BUT WHAT I HAVE TO KNOW IS WHO GAVE THE ORDER?
WHO SET ME UP?
WHO SENT ME TO HELL?
AND IF I'M DEAD, HOW COME I HAVE A BODY? SINCE WHEN DID DEAD GUYS GET TO HAVE BODIES?
AND IF I'M HERE, WHAT DID THEY BURY IN AL SIMMONS' GRAVE?

THERE'S ONLY ONE WAY TO FIND OUT.
I KNOW WHERE I HAVE TO GO EVEN THOUGH IT SCARES THE CRAP OUT OF ME. THERE'S SOMETHING I SHOULD HAVE DONE A LONG TIME AGO.
BUT FIRST I NEED TO LET OFF SOME STEAM.
MAYBE SPREAD A LITTLE OF THIS PAIN AROUND.
BACK OFF, GUYS.
WELL, WHAT HAVE WE GOT HERE?
ONE MORE PIECE OF GARBAGE THAT DIDN'T GET SWEPT AWAY. I DUNNO WHAT THIS CITY'S COMIN' TO, I REALLY DON'T.
I DON'T REALLY THINK YOU WANT TO DO THIS...
OH YEAH. WELL, I DON'T GIVE A FLYIN' FART WHAT YOU THINK, SCUMBAG.
WE'RE JUST A COUPLE OF CONCERNED CITIZENS TRYIN' TO DO SOMETHIN' ABOUT THE HOMELESS PROBLEM. WE CALL IT THE 'BURN A BUM' SCHEME, DON'T WE BERNIE?
'BURN A BUM.' HUR HUR HUR
SOLINE

SO GET READY TO BURN IN HELL, 'CAUSE...
UH?
HELL?
THEN LET'S TALK.
JEEZ! IT'S THAT GUY! THE SPAWN GUY! THE SPOOK!
YOU REALLY WANT TO TALK ABOUT HELL, BUD?
BLOW HIM AWAY, BERNIE!
YOU HEARD HIM, BERNIE. GO AHEAD.
BLOW ME AWAY.
MY HAND! ...YOU'RE... ah...

LOOKS LIKE BERNIE'S TOO BUSY RIGHT NOW.
YOU WANT TO TAKE A SHOT?
SCUM!
JESUS, GIMME A BREAK. WE WEREN'T GONNA TORCH THE GUY. IT WAS JUST A JOKE...
IT'S NOT FAIR... USIN' POWERS AGAINST NORMAL GUYS...
YOU THINK I NEED POWERS TO DEAL WITH SCUM LIKE YOU?
DO YOU?
...NNNNNZZ
NNNNNGGGG
...MY HAND...

SORRY ABOUT THAT. GUESS I WAS JUST FEELING PISSED.
GUESS YOU WERE.
I KNOW IT'S HARD 'ROUND HERE BUT TRY TO KEEP OUT OF TROUBLE.
AND IF ANYONE COMES LOOKING FOR ME, TELL THEM I'VE GONE TO DIG UP AN OLD FRIEND.
SURE I WILL, HELLSPAWN.
SURE I WILL.

NOT FAR AWAY, IN MIDTOWN MANHATTAN, IN A MIRROR-WALLED BUILDING WITH NO NAME AND NO NUMBER...
WELL, IF WE'VE HAD TO WITHDRAW OUR DIPLOMATIC ENVOY FROM HELL THE PROBLEM IS SERIOUS, YES. YES, I UNDER-STAND.
RIGHT AWAY... YES.
...I WOULD NEVER QUESTION A DIRECT ORDER, NO, BUT ISN'T THIS A LITTLE ...WELL, DRASTIC?
I'VE DONE MY BEST TO RUN TERRAN AFFAIRS QUIETLY AND WITHOUT...
PROBLEMS, GABRIELLE?
NEW ORDERS FROM UPSTAIRS. REMEMBER THE EARTHBOUND HELL-SPAWN WHO DEFEATED ANGELA RECENTLY?
WELL, APPARENTLY THIS SPAWN IS SPECIAL AND SPECIAL MEANS DANGEROUS. WE'VE BEEN EMPOWERED TO CREATE OUR OWN SOLDIER TO DESTROY THE CREATURE.
THE BALANCE OF POWER MUST BE SERIOUSLY COMPRO-MISED IF CONTROL'S PREPARED TO INTERVENE SO DIRECTLY IN THE AFFAIRS OF THE EARTHLY PLANE.
LET'S JUST HOPE OUR ORBITAL ANGEL STATION IS UP AND RUNNING, MICHAELA.
WE HAVE WORK TO DO.

...THAT'S THE SITUATION AS IT STANDS. WE HAVE FULL AUTHORITY TO EMPOWER A HUMAN AGENT TO DESTROY THE HELLSPAWN.
IS THE STATION READY?
OF COURSE. IT WAS A SIMPLE MATTER TO HOLLOW OUT THE BODIES OF THE HUMANS HERE AND INSTALL OUR OWN ESSENCES WITHIN THEM.
THIS STATION IS NOW FULLY OPERATIONAL, GABRIELLE.
WE WILL BEGIN THE PROCEDURE IMMEDIATELY.
I WILL CONTACT THE AVENGING ANGEL OF THE FIFTH HEAVEN AND ARRANGE FOR THE TRANSFER OF THE ELEMENTAL FIRE.
YOUR SOLDIER WILL BE FULLY EMPOWERED AND READY FOR COMBAT BEFORE SUNRISE YOUR TIME.
A SOLDIER?
FEARFUL TIMES ARE UPON US, IT SEEMS.
WHAT KIND OF HUMAN HAS THE STRENGTH TO BEAR THE ELEMENTAL FIRE?
THE SUBJECT HAS ALREADY BEEN SELECTED.
I'M BRINGING HIM UP NOW.

READY WHEN YOU ARE, GENTLEMEN.
WOK
SKRAK

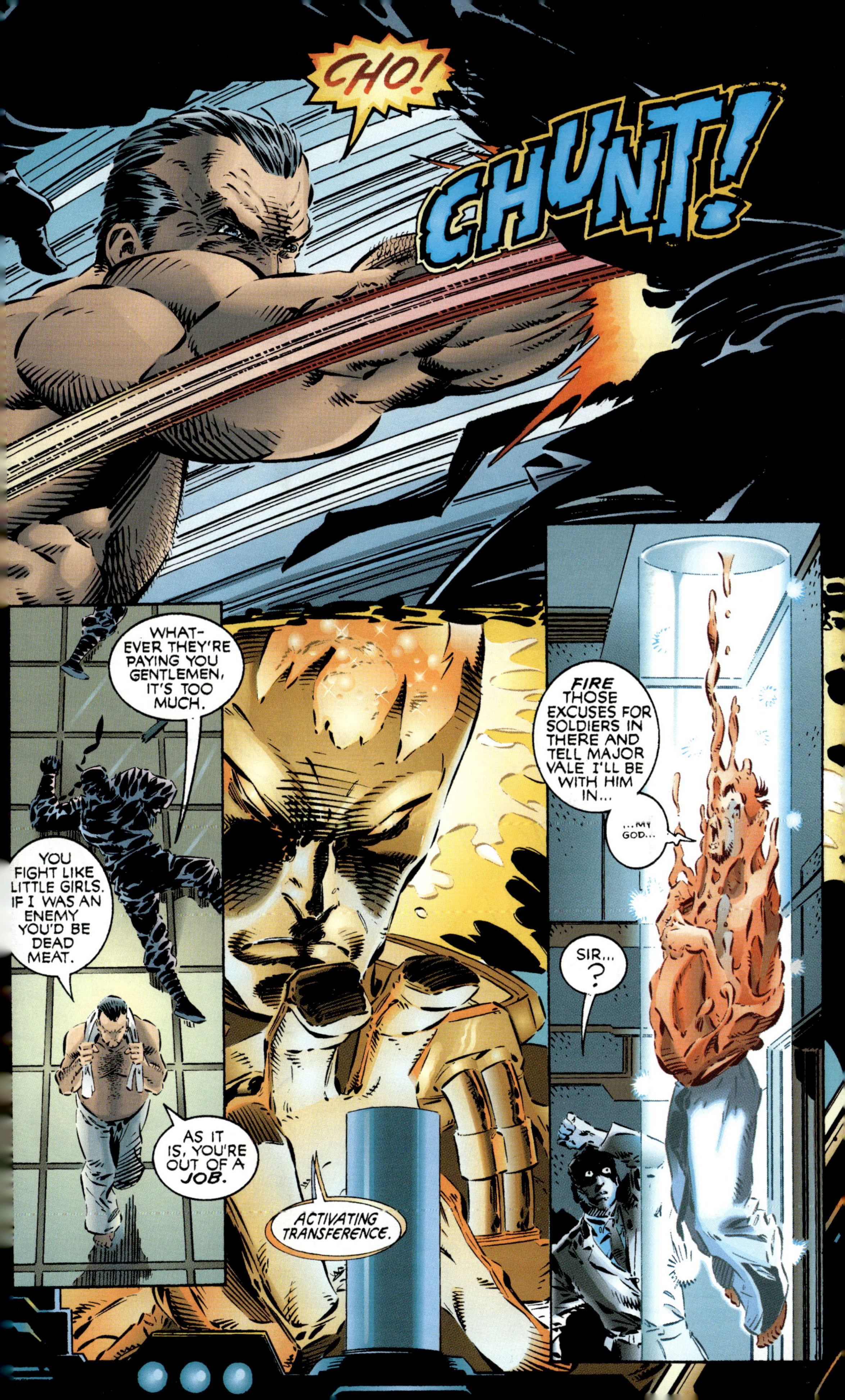

CHO!
CHUNT!
WHATEVER THEY'RE PAYING YOU GENTLEMEN, IT'S TOO MUCH.
YOU FIGHT LIKE LITTLE GIRLS. IF I WAS AN ENEMY YOU'D BE DEAD MEAT.
AS IT IS, YOU'RE OUT OF A JOB.
ACTIVATING TRANSFERENCE.
FIRE THOSE EXCUSES FOR SOLDIERS IN THERE AND TELL MAJOR VALE I'LL BE WITH HIM IN...
...MY GOD...
SIR...?

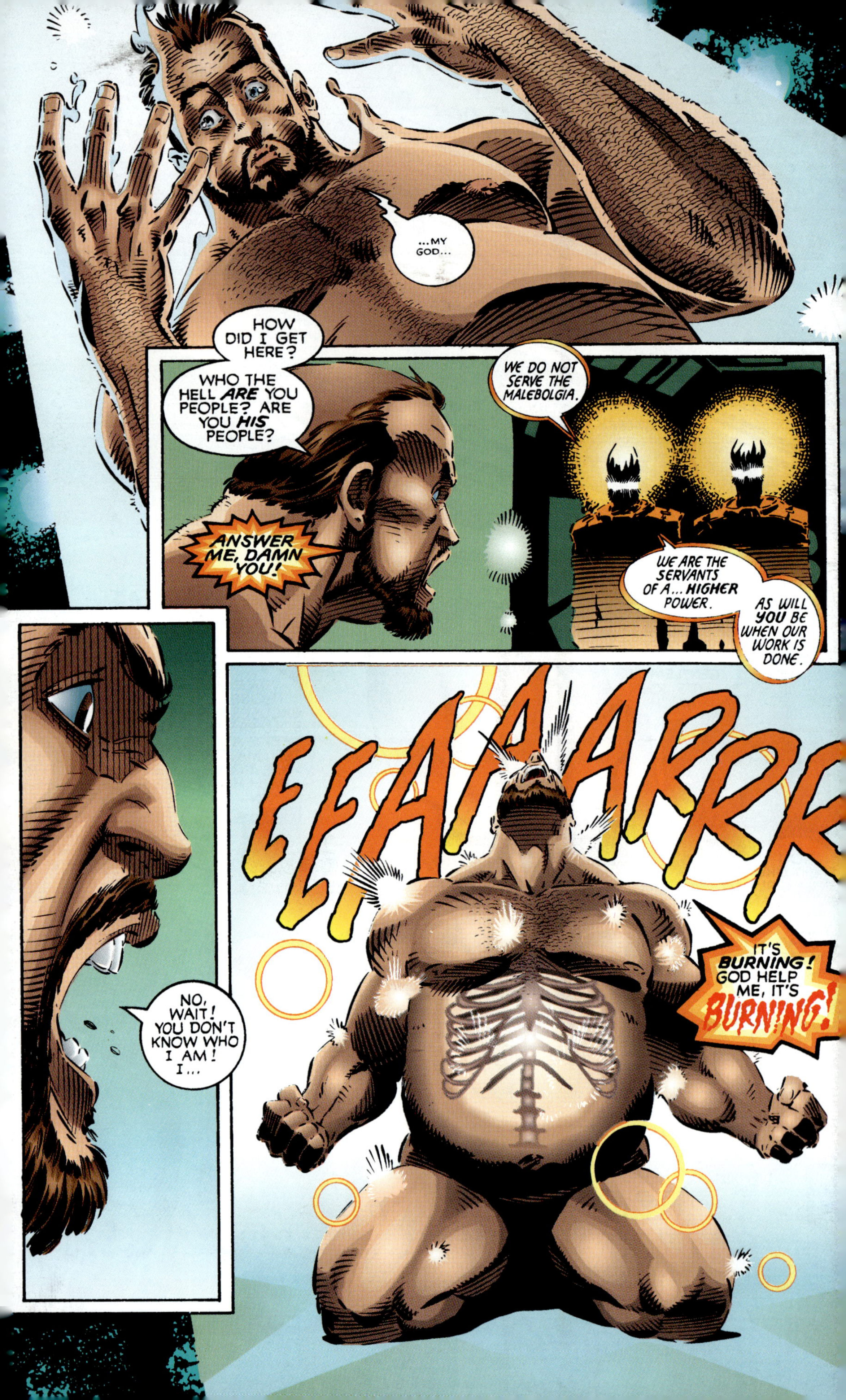

...MY GOD...
HOW DID I GET HERE?
WHO THE HELL ARE YOU PEOPLE? ARE YOU HIS PEOPLE?
WE DO NOT SERVE THE MALEBOLGIA.
ANSWER ME, DAMN YOU!
WE ARE THE SERVANTS OF A... HIGHER POWER.
AS WILL YOU BE WHEN OUR WORK IS DONE.
EFAP ARRK
NO, WAIT! YOU DON'T KNOW WHO I AM! I...
IT'S BURNING! GOD HELP ME, IT'S BURNING!

THIS IS THE PLACE.
WHAT AM I SO SCARED OF?
THERE WON'T BE ANYTHING IN HERE.
SIMMONS
THIS IS WHERE THEY BURIED ME.
THERE CAN'T BE.
THEY CAN'T HAVE BURIED AL SIMMONS HERE BECAUSE I'M AL SIMMONS.

I'LL PULL BACK THE LID OF THIS GODDAMN COFFIN AND I'LL LOOK IN AND I'LL SEE...
No.
NO!
THE SMELL! LIKE SOME SICK, ANCIENT THING BREATHING IN MY FACE... FILTHY... ROTTEN...
IT'S ME. DEAR GOD IN HEAVEN, IT'S MY BODY.
AND IF THIS... THIS THING IS ALL THAT'S LEFT OF AL SIMMONS...
WHAT AM I? GOD HELP ME...
WHAT AM I?
WHAT HAVE YOU DONE TO ME?

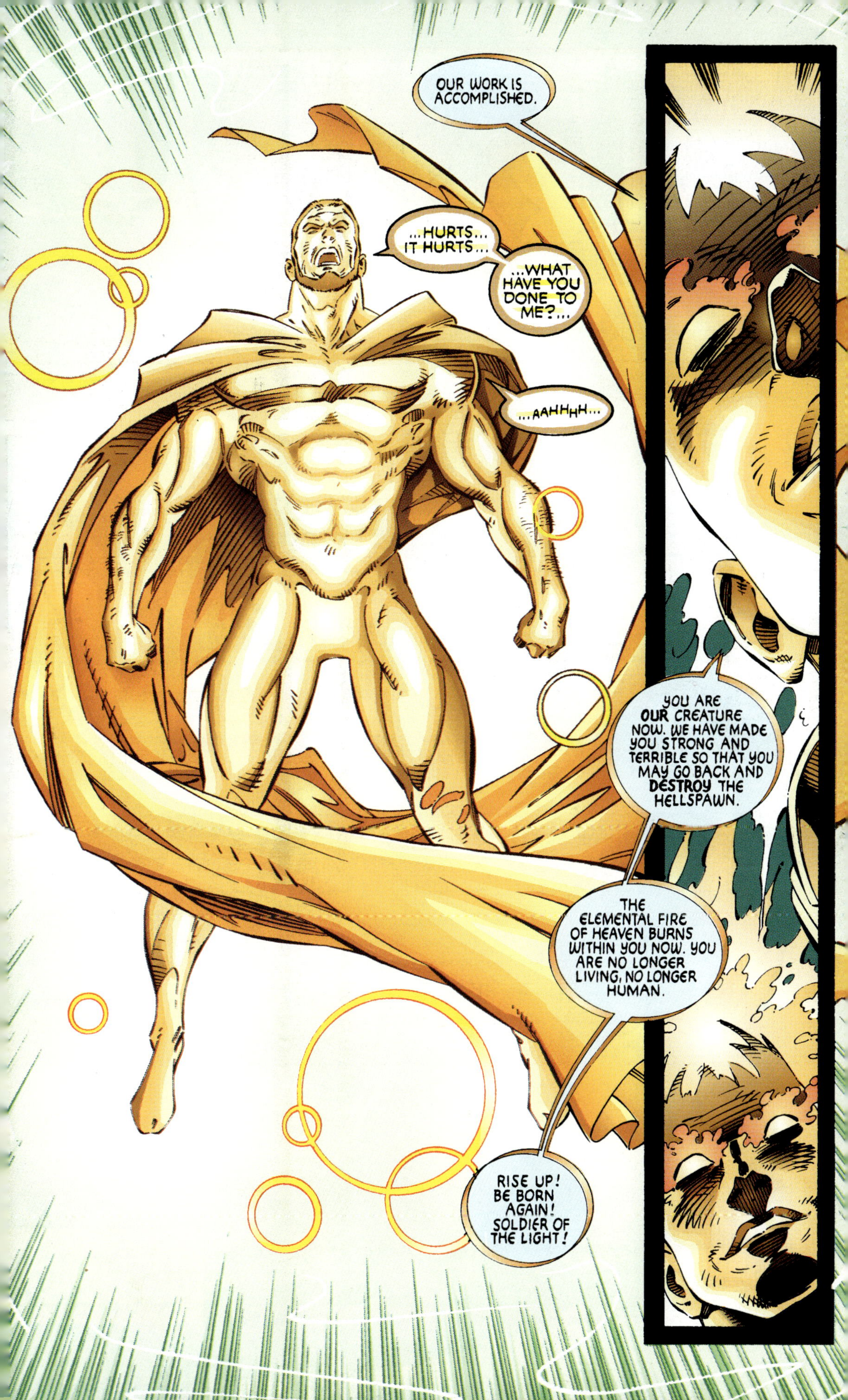

OUR WORK IS ACCOMPLISHED.
...HURTS... IT HURTS...
...WHAT HAVE YOU DONE TO ME?...
...AAHHHH...
YOU ARE OUR CREATURE NOW. WE HAVE MADE YOU STRONG AND TERRIBLE SO THAT YOU MAY GO BACK AND DESTROY THE HELLSPAWN.
THE ELEMENTAL FIRE OF HEAVEN BURNS WITHIN YOU NOW. YOU ARE NO LONGER LIVING, NO LONGER HUMAN.
RISE UP! BE BORN AGAIN! SOLDIER OF THE LIGHT!

ANTI-SPAWN!
AAAAHHH
NEXT
MALEBOLGIA
IS THE DEVIL!

F L E C T I O N S

SOMEWHERE IN TIME, THERE IS LAUGHTER...
HA HA HA
HA HA
HA HA HA
THE MOCKING, MIRTHLESS LAUGHTER OF THE BAD GOD, THE MALBOLGIA, AS HE SURVEYS HIS WORK AND DECLARES IT GOOD...
...AS HE GAZES DOWN UPON THE MAN HE HAS CONDEMNED TO AN UNLIVING HELL.
HIS CREATURE, HIS KNIGHT OF THE PIT...

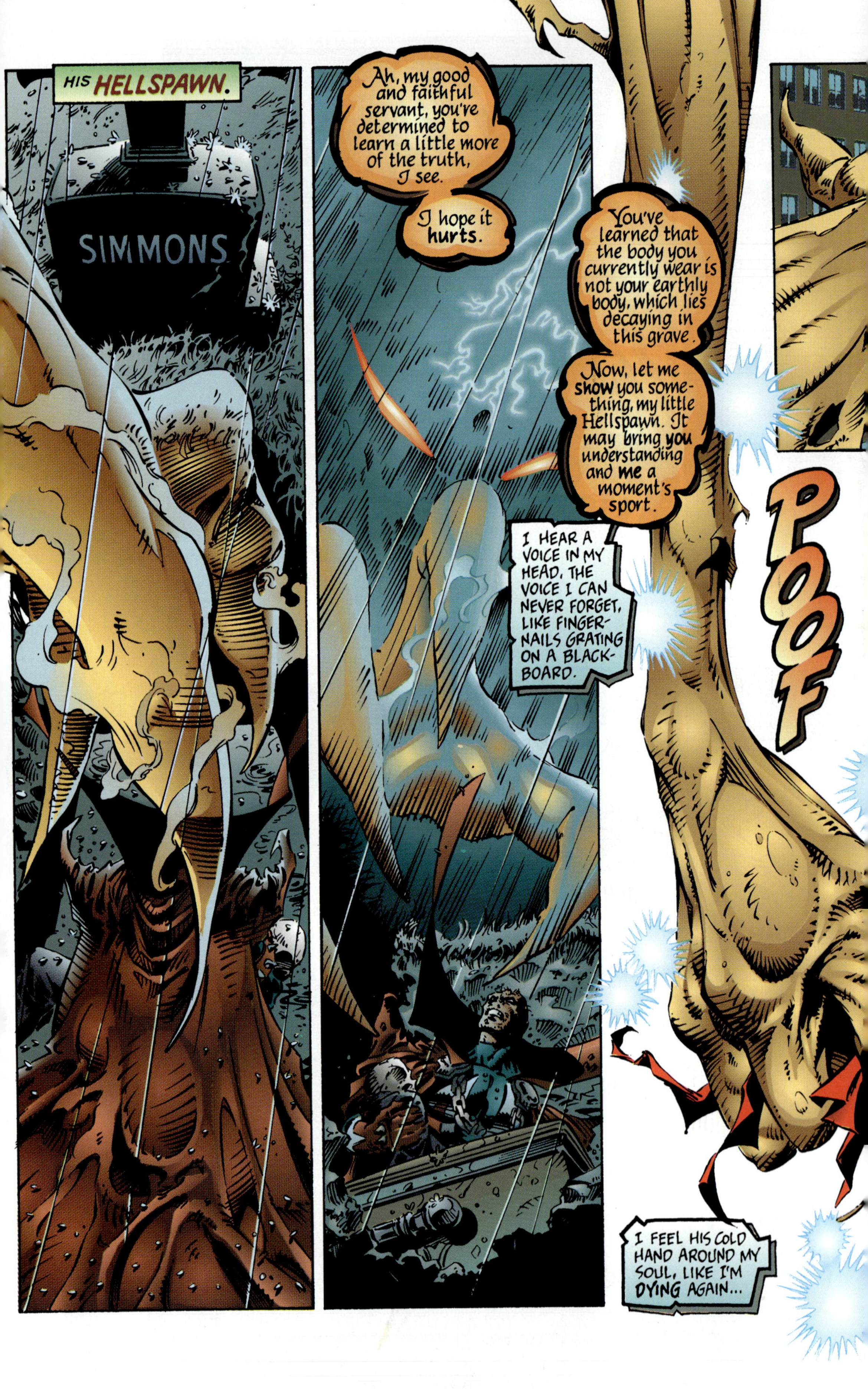

HIS HELLSPAWN.
SIMMONS
Ah, my good and faithful servant, you're determined to learn a little more of the truth, I see.
I hope it hurts.
You've learned that the body you currently wear is not your earthly body, which lies decaying in this grave.
Now, let me show you something, my little Hellspawn. It may bring you understanding and me a moment's sport.
I HEAR A VOICE IN MY HEAD, THE VOICE I CAN NEVER FORGET, LIKE FINGERNAILS GRATING ON A BLACKBOARD.
POOF
I FEEL HIS COLD HAND AROUND MY SOUL, LIKE I'M DYING AGAIN...

AND SUDDENLY, I'M SOMEWHERE ELSE, AWAY FROM THE RAIN.
WHERE AM I?
This place is a doorway into my realm, a gate that stands open onto Hell. This particular portal occupies part of a military testing ground in Nevada.
Surely, you recognize what you see?
THIS STREET... I LIVED HERE WHEN I WAS A KID... THAT CHURCH IS WHERE I WAS MARRIED...
MY GOD, WHAT IS THIS PLACE?
How kind of you to call me God.
Hell is built of a substance your people have taken to calling psychoplasm, which adapts itself to human thoughts and fears.
When you died, your memories acted upon psychoplasm to create all of this.
Just as your new Spawn body is composed of psychoplasm and can change its shape, so too can this gateway assume the forms of any thoughts or emotions imprinted upon it.
Look! Do you remember that day on the lake, when you bent the knee and begged Wanda to marry you? How touching...
NOOOOOO
Not your wife, just a stray memory given flesh. But how such memories must sting when you think of her in the arms of another man!
Oh, I delight in the sweet, sad taste of your pain, little Hellspawn. For you, there can be only pain. I savor the bitterness of your tears on my tongue.
Each day, you are more my slave. It will not be long before you crawl towards my throne to take your place in my army.
I look forward to seeing you.
HAHAHA HAHA
WANDA? NO, LEAVE HER OUT OF THIS... NOT MY WIFE.

SOMEWHERE IN TIME, THERE IS LAUGHTER. BUT THE BAD GOD DOES NOT LAUGH ALONE. THERE IS ANOTHER SOUND IN THE AIRLESS DARK...
THE COLD LAUGHTER OF ANGELS.
IT IS DONE.
THE SOLDIER IS READY. OUR ANTI-SPAWN HAS BEEN PREPARED FOR HIS FIRST BATTLE.
THEN KEY HIM TO THE HELLSPAWN'S AURA PROFILE, INITIATE TRANSMISSION.
AND PRAY FOR A SWIFT KILL.
THERE IS A BRIEF SOUND, LIKE A CHOIR CATCHING ITS BREATH, AND A SILVER WHITE COMET EXPLODES DOWN THROUGH THE UPPER ATMOSPHERE.

WHERE ARE YOU, YOU BASTARD ?!
YOU TOOK MY LIFE, YOU TOOK MY SOUL !
WHERE ARE YOU ?! I...
WHOOOM
DON'T KNOW WHAT THE HELL THAT WAS BUT MY SKIN'S CRAWLING WITH STATIC.
THERE'S SOMETHING IN THERE...

SOMETHING BAD.
HELLSPAWN!
I'VE COME FOR YOU!

...MEANWHILE, IN WASHINGTON, GOVERNMENT SOURCES ARE REFUSING TO CONFIRM OR DENY RUMORS ABOUT THE DIS-APPEARANCE OF CONTROVERCIAL PRESIDENTIAL ADVISOR JASON WYNN.
WYNN WAS SCHEDULED TO APPEAR IN A LIVE TELEVISION DEBATE EARLIER
CNN
KLIK

OTHER VIEWS
...CAN CALL ME A CRANK ALL THEY WANT BUT I SAY THE WHOLE WYNN DISAPPEARANCE STORY STINKS TO HIGH HEAVEN OF CONSPIRACY AND COVER-UP!
JUST WHAT WERE WYNN'S CONNECTIONS TO ALLEGED YOUNGBLOOD COVERT OPERATIONS AND ALL THOSE OTHER SNEAKY LITTLE DIRTY-TRICKS OUTINGS THAT NOBODY SEEMS TO WANT TO REPORT?

AND WHAT DID WYNN HAVE TO SAY ABOUT THE NEW INFORMATION THAT'S COME TO LIGHT WHICH SUGGESTS THAT LT. COL. AL SIMMONS, WHO DIED SIX YEARS AGO, MAY HAVE BEEN MURDERED BY HIS OWN PEOPLE?
PRETTY STRANGE THEN THAT JASON WYNN SHOULD SUDDENLY
KLIK

...BEST FOR YOUR DOG, BEST FOR YOUR POCKET.
WAS THAT SOMETHING ON THE NEWS ABOUT AL?
UH... NOT REALLY. THEY'RE STILL TALKING ABOUT THIS JASON WYNN THING. I DIDN'T THINK YOU'D WANT TO HEAR IT AGAIN, WANDA...

I NEVER LIKED THAT GUY, WYNN.
HE CAME AROUND A COUPLE OF TIMES WHEN AL AND I WERE MARRIED AND HE ALWAYS GAVE ME THE CREEPS.
WELL, JASON WAS INVOLVED IN A LOT OF BAD STUFF BUT HE ALWAYS MANAGED TO KEEP HIS NOSE CLEAN.
I GUESS THAT'S WHY AL FINALLY FELL OUT WITH HIM.
IT'S WEIRD, YOU KNOW... I KEEP THINKING ABOUT AL. IT'S... WELL, IT'S LIKE HE WAS SOMEHOW THERE IN A WAY THAT HE WASN'T BEFORE... I DON'T KNOW...
IT'S KIND OF SPOOKY, I GUESS.
AS LONG AS YOU DON'T STOP THINKING ABOUT ME, HONEY.
NOT IN A MILLION YEARS, TERRY. YOU KNOW THAT.
AND WHO KNOWS ABOUT JASON WYNN OR WHETHER HE'S VANISHED OFF THE FACE OF THE EARTH ANYWAY?
I MEAN, DOES IT REALLY MATTER?
MORE THAN YOU THINK, WANDA BLAKE...
KLIK

...FOR JASON WYNN HAS BEEN REBORN AS THE ANTI-SPAWN AND STANDS FACE TO FACE WITH HIS OLD ADVERSARY, AL SIMMONS--
--THOUGH NEITHER MAN SUSPECTS.
YEAH?
YOU'RE WELCOME TO TRY.
I'VE COME TO DESTROY YOU, HELLSPAWN.
SHRAAK

WHATEVER HE THROWS AT ME, IT HITS LIKE A FREIGHT TRAIN.
FEELS LIKE EVERYTHING INSIDE ME JUST CAUGHT FIRE. LIKE HOT GLASS AND ACID IN MY VEINS. EVERYTHING SPINS AND A WALL COMES UP BEHIND ME. COLORS...
SKRASSSSH

UNNH!
LIGHTNING CRACKLING DOWN MY NERVOUS SYSTEM.
I CAN SMELL INCENSE AND OLD WOOD... HURT BAD... THIS IS WHERE WE WERE MARRIED... WANDA... BUT IT'S NOT A CHURCH, IS IT? ... JUST HELL PRETENDING TO BE A CHURCH...
GOD, I'M IN AGONY!
AND THOSE VOICES SURE AIN'T CHOIRBOYS...
LOOKEE HERE WHAT WE GOT?
IS IT A HELLSPAWN? SMELLS LIKE A HELLSPAWN.
IT'S A HELLSPAWN ALL RIGHT. NOT SO HIGH AND MIGHTY NOW, IS HE?
LET'S SEE HIM ORDER US AROUND.
I GOT AN IDEA. LET'S TAKE HIS UNIFORM WHILE IT'S STILL STUNNED. NO REASON WHY WE SHOULDN'T BE FINE CAPTAINS IN HELL'S ARMY.
WON'T THE UNIFORM BE BONDED TO HIS NERVOUS SYSTEM?

NOT ONCE WE'VE PEELED HIM LIKE A
WHUMMP!
STAND AWAY FROM HIM!
HE'S MINE!
FILTH! DO YOU HEAR ME?
HE'S MINE!

EEE EE
EEAAA
STINK OF BURNING MEAT AND SULFUR.
WHO IS THIS GUY? NEVER FACED SO MUCH RAW POWER. WHAT THE HELL DOES HE WANT?
WHAT IF HE'S STRONGER THAN ME?
AND HOW COME I FEEL LIKE I KNOW HIM?
SEE? SEE HOW THE HOLY BURNING LIGHT OF HEAVEN DISPELS THE DARKNESS?
NOW YOU, HELLSPAWN.
I'LL MAKE YOU SCREAM.

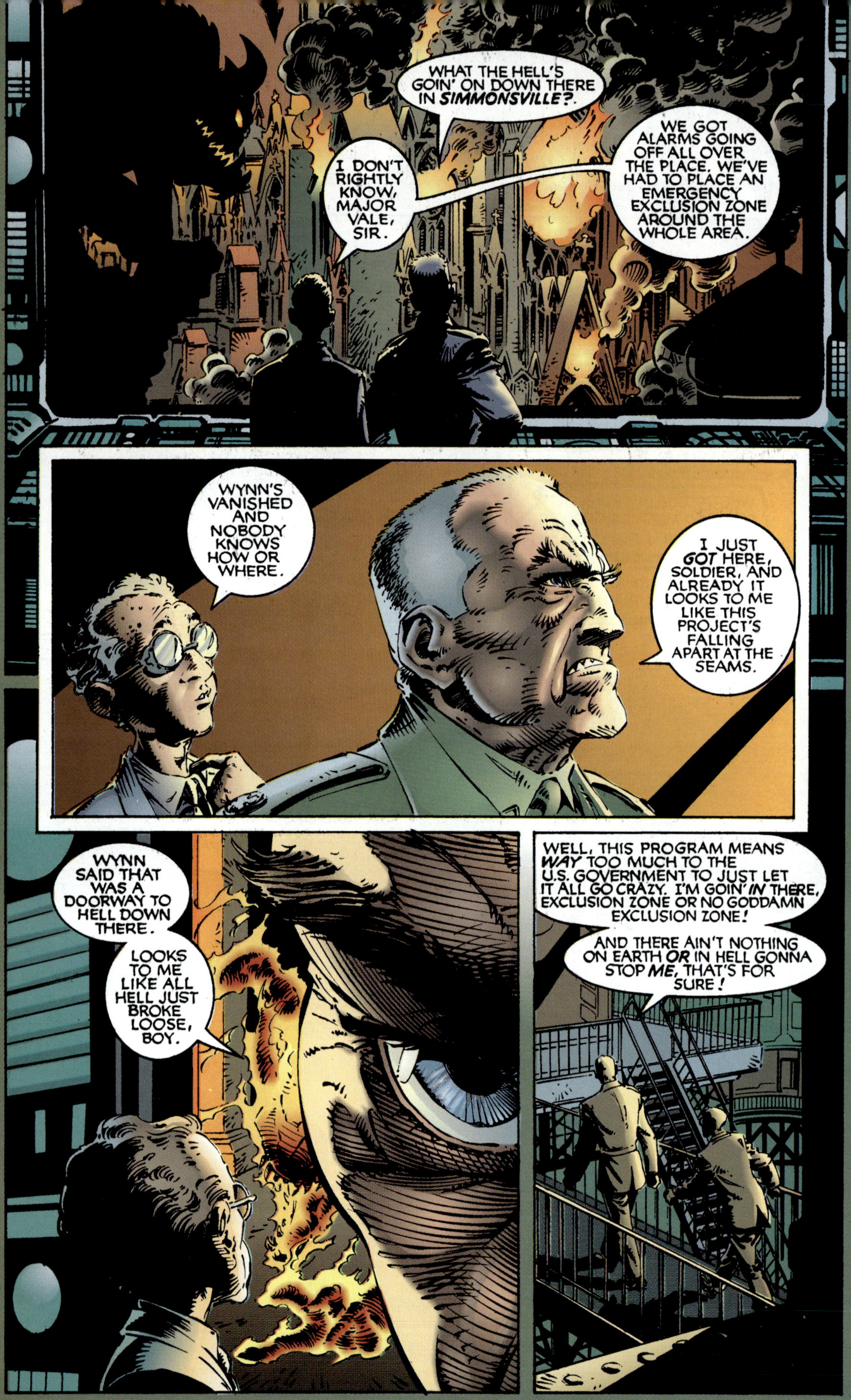

WHAT THE HELL'S GOIN' ON DOWN THERE IN SIMMONSVILLE?.
I DON'T RIGHTLY KNOW, MAJOR VALE, SIR.
WE GOT ALARMS GOING OFF ALL OVER THE PLACE. WE'VE HAD TO PLACE AN EMERGENCY EXCLUSION ZONE AROUND THE WHOLE AREA.
WYNN'S VANISHED AND NOBODY KNOWS HOW OR WHERE.
I JUST GOT HERE, SOLDIER, AND ALREADY IT LOOKS TO ME LIKE THIS PROJECT'S FALLING APART AT THE SEAMS.
WYNN SAID THAT WAS A DOORWAY TO HELL DOWN THERE.
LOOKS TO ME LIKE ALL HELL JUST BROKE LOOSE, BOY.
WELL, THIS PROGRAM MEANS WAY TOO MUCH TO THE U.S. GOVERNMENT TO JUST LET IT ALL GO CRAZY. I'M GOIN' IN THERE, EXCLUSION ZONE OR NO GODDAMN EXCLUSION ZONE!
AND THERE AIN'T NOTHING ON EARTH OR IN HELL GONNA STOP ME, THAT'S FOR SURE!

I CAN'T TAKE MUCH MORE OF THIS.
GOT TO TRY AND TAKE HIM OUT.
GODDAMN! I MISSED!
I MISSED AND HE'S STILL COMING.
SHRAAAK!

THE NEXT BLAST WILL KILL ME.
GOTTA GET OUT OF HERE.
A SWITCH SNAPS HOME IN MY BRAIN AND I DISSOLVE MY BODY.
EVERYTHING FALLS INWARD, LIKE A COLLAPSING BALLOON. THE WORLD BREAKS UP AND GOES OUT.
AND I'M TRAVELLING.
A SHOTGUN BLAST THROUGH UN-SPACE AT THE SPEED OF LIGHT. STRESSED MOLECULES SHRIEKING WITH SHOCK.
I'M NEVER GONNA BELIEVE ANYTHING I SEE ON 'STAR TREK' AGAIN; TELEPORTATION HURTS.
IT HURTS BAD.

AND, AS BEFORE, THE SPAWN IS DRAWN BACK, AS THOUGH BY SOME PSYCHIC MAGNET, TO THE LABYRINTHINE ALLEYWAYS OF THE BOWERY...
...TO THE PLACE HE CALLS HOME.
SO I SAYS TO THE COP, I SAYS... HEY! LOOKIT THIS HERE!
WHATCHA CALL THAT?!
JEE-ZUS! IT'S THE FOURTH OF JULY!
GET AWAY... ALL OF YOU... HE MIGHT BE ABLE TO FOLLOW...
GET AWAY!
IT'S THE SPAWN! YOU DON'T LOOK SO GOOD, BIG GUY...
NO! GET OUT OF HERE!
GO!
IT CAN'T BE... HE CAN'T HAVE COME AFTER ME SO SOON.
I NEED MORE TIME...

YOU CAN'T HIDE. I CAN TRACK YOU THROUGH TIME AND SPACE, TO THE ENDS OF THE EARTH!
THERE'S NOWHERE TO RUN FROM DEATH!
SKRAAAK

CAN'T SEE STRAIGHT... EVERYTHING BROKEN UP INSIDE. IS THAT BLOOD IN MY EYES, OR...
...JESUS, THAT NOISE... IT'S MY COSTUME! BLEEDING... MOANING...
MY COSTUME'S ALIVE AND HE'S WOUNDED IT...
DON'T YOU UNDERSTAND THE PAIN? BURNING INSIDE... WHITE FIRE... THEY SET LIGHT TO MY SOUL...
IF I KILL YOU, THE ANGELS WILL LET ME REST.
ANGELS? WHAT'S HE TALKING ABOUT?
I'M LOSING CONSCIOUSNESS.
CAN'T TAKE ANOTHER...

SHRRZZZZ
UUUHHHH H

HEAD'S FILLED WITH LIGHT... I CAN'T THINK STRAIGHT... I JUST HAVE TO KILL YOU...
THEN THE FIRES WILL GO OUT. I WAS A MAN ONCE... WAS I A MAN? NOW I'M THE FIERY SOLDIER OF HEAVEN... HEAVEN'S HUNTER, HEAVEN'S HARRIER AND YOU...
YOU'RE JUST PREY!
SHIIIING!

TIME'S UP, HELLSPAWN!

SPAWN
IMAGE
18
FEB
$1.95
$2.95 Canada

ON THE STREET THEY CALL HIM DIPPER.
NO.
THIS AIN'T RIGHT.
HE WASN'T ALWAYS DIPPER; HE USED TO BE SOMEONE ELSE.
MARTY. THAT WAS IT. MARTY SLADEK.
PRIVATE MARTY SLADEK. KHE SANH. '69.
'YOU GOTTA WATCH OUT FOR YOUR BUDDIES.' THAT WAS THE RULE IN 'NAM.
ONLY ONE TIME, HE DIDN'T...
HE STILL DREAMS ABOUT IT-- THE HOT WIND LIKE A PUNCH IN THE GUT AND THE FLYING CHUNKS OF WET MEAT THAT USED TO BE MEN.
HE'D FELT THAT SAME DEVIL'S WIND AGAIN WHEN THE SHINING GUY TOOK OUT THE SPAWN, JUST MOMENTS AGO.
WHAT'S A GUY TO DO?
WHAT'S A GUY TO DO WHEN HE'S SEEN HIS BEST BUDDIES TURNED INTO EXHIBITS FROM A MUSEUM OF HORRORS?
THEY ROTATED MARTY BACK TO THE WORLD BUT IT DIDN'T MAKE SENSE ANYMORE. HE JUST KEPT DRINKING AND DRINKING UNTIL HE FORGOT WHY HE EVER STARTED.
BUT NOW IT'S HAPPENING AGAIN.
THE SPAWN GUY TURNED UP OUT OF NOWHERE WITH SOME SUPER-CRAZY ON HIS TAIL. HE WAS BEATEN, WIPED-OUT, AND NOBODY SEEMED ABLE TO DO ANYTHING TO HELP.
'YOU GOTTA WATCH OUT FOR YOUR BUDDIES.' THAT WAS THE RULE.
IT AIN'T RIGHT WE SHOULD JUST STAND HERE.
IT JUST AIN'T RIGHT.
BUT THAT WAS A LONG TIME AGO.

AND THIS IS NOW.
SEE, HELLSPAWN?
IT'S EASY TO DIE.

I PROMISE TO MAKE IT HURT.
WHACANG
YOU GOTTA WATCH OUT FOR YOUR BUDDIES.
WHO...?

FILTH!
I'LL BURN YOUR EYES OUT! I'LL--
I DON'T THINK SO, PAL.
THIS IS OUR TURF AND WE STICK TOGETHER.
YOU GOT A BEEF WITH THE SPAWN YOU GOT A BEEF WITH ALL OF US.

YOU DON'T KNOW WHAT YOU'RE FACING...
I'LL TEAR YOU ALL APART...
THAT'S ENOUGH, BUD.
THESE PEOPLE ARE UNDER MY PROTECTION.

GOT THAT?
KROOM

SHRAAAAK!
MY COSTUME HOWLS AS HE TAGS ME WITH ANOTHER BLAST.
GOT TO MOVE IN FAST.

I'M STILL WEAK.

I CAN'T AFFORD TO LET HIM GAIN THE ADVANTAGE AGAIN.

I'LL SHOW YOU PAIN.
THIS IS WHAT I FEEL.

YOU THINK YOU CAN HURT ME-- HEAVEN'S SOLDIER?

NNNGH

RRRRAAAA
WHOK!
FEELS LIKE LIVE WIRES...
BURNING LIGHTS IN MY
HEAD... JESUS, DON'T
LET ME PASS OUT...
WHUNCH!
IT LOOKS LIKE HE'S EXPENDED
TOO MUCH ENERGY. MAYBE HIS
POWERS ARE SIMILAR TO MINE.
NO TIME TO THINK
ABOUT THAT NOW.
I HAVE TO FINISH
THIS.
I'LL KILL YOU...
YEAH?

WELCOME TO THE REAL WORLD, BASTARD!
HAVE A NICE DAY.
TSCHH!

AAAAHHHH

I'LL KILL YOU... I'LL KILL YOU...

TELL ME ABOUT IT.

I THINK I GOT HIM.
I HIT HIM. SCARED THE CRAP OUTTA ME BUT I HIT HIM.
YOU GOTTA WATCH OUT FOR YOUR BUDDIES, RIGHT?
DID I DO THE RIGHT THING?
SURE, DIPPER.
YOU DID THE RIGHT THING, BUDDY.
JEEZ! WHAT'S HE DOIN' NOW?
DISAPPEARED. LOOK AT THAT.
WELL, I'LL BE DAMNED.
I WOULDN'T RECOMMEND IT.

HIGH ABOVE THE EARTH ORBITS THE ANGEL STATION, SOURCE OF THE ANTI-SPAWN'S HEAVENLY POWER...
CONTROL MAY SEE THIS AS A FAILURE ON OUR PART.
IT WAS A FIRST TEST RUN, NOTHING MORE. THE HELLSPAWN IS STRONGER AND MORE RESOURCEFUL THAN WE HAD THOUGHT.
WE MUST INCREASE OUR SOLDIER'S POWER LEVELS AND PREPARE HIM MORE THOROUGHLY FOR FUTURE ENCOUNTERS.
RELEASE ME... PLEASE... I'M BURNING INSIDE...
KILL ME...
MORE ELEMENTAL FIRE!
NO MORE! PLEASE!
NOOOOO

I DON'T KNOW WHAT THE HELL THAT WAS ALL ABOUT BUT I HOPE IT'S OVER...
WELL, I HEARD YOU COULD BE PRETTY DUMB BUT GIMME A BREAK! OVER?
YOU THINK HEAVEN GOES TO ALL THE TROUBLE OF EMPOWERING AN ANTI-SPAWN JUST TO HAVE IT BEATEN IN ONE LITTLE SCUFFLE?

AN ANTI-SPAWN?
LOOK, WHO ARE YOU? DIDN'T I SEE YOU EARLIER?
SURE DID. YOU EVEN SAVED MY LIFE, ALTHOUGH, TO TELL THE TRUTH, IT DIDN'T NEED SAVING.
WE'VE BEEN WATCHING YOU, SIMMONS. I BELIEVE YOU MET ONE OF US BEFORE, A MAN NAMED CAGLIOSTRO.*
YOU SEE, HEAVEN AND HELL AIN'T THE ONLY PLAYERS IN THIS GAME.
THERE ARE OTHER POWERS AND AGENCIES, OWING ALLEGIANCE TO NEITHER SIDE, AND THERE ARE METHODS WHEREBY YOU CAN UNDO THE BARGAIN YOU MADE AND RETAIN YOUR POWERS.
BELIEVE ME, YOU CAN BEAT THE DEVIL.
WHO ARE YOU?
WHAT ARE YOU TELLING ME?
*SEE ISSUE #9 -- Tom

MY CARD.

BUT...
BUT IT'S
BLANK.

ONLY
FOR
NOW.

WHEN
THE TIME
COMES,
WE'LL BE IN
TOUCH.

MORE
QUESTIONS.

FOR
ANOTHER
DAY.

RIGHT NOW, THERE'S
SOMETHING I STILL
HAVE TO DO.

HERE IN THE NEVADA DESERT, THERE'S A DOORWAY TO HELL. IT LOOKS LIKE A TOWN BUT IT'S MADE OUT OF SOMETHING CALLED PSYCHOPLASM-- A SUBSTANCE WHICH CHANGES SHAPE IN RESPONSE TO THOUGHTS AND EMOTIONS.
THEY TOOK MY MEMORIES AND USED THEM TO GIVE FORM TO THIS TERRIBLE PLACE.
THEY TOOK EVERYTHING I WAS AND PERVERTED IT.
NOW I'M TAKIN' IT BACK.
KA CHAKK
WHOOOOM

ONLY WAY I KNOW HOW.
YOU THERE!
STOP RIGHT THERE!
TURN AROUND! SHOW YOURSELF, GODDAMNIT!
Oh GOD.
WHO ARE YOU?...
WELL, WELL. YOU WON'T REMEMBER ME BUT I REMEMBER YOU, MAJOR VALE. YOU AND JASON WYNN WERE CUT FROM THE SAME CLOTH, WEREN'T YOU?
REMEMBER ECUADOR? SIX GOOD MEN DIED. A WHOLE VILLAGE OF INNOCENT PEOPLE WAS WIPED OUT AND YOU AND JASON COVERED THE WHOLE THING UP.
HOW DO YOU KNOW ABOUT THAT? THAT WAS A COVERT OPERATION. WHO THE HELL ARE YOU, MISTER?
ANSWER ME! THAT'S AN ORDER!
MAYBE I GOT SICK OF TAKING ORDERS FROM PEOPLE LIKE YOU, VALE.
NOW I'M GIVING YOU AN ORDER.

DROP DEAD.
I WISH I COULD SAY IT MAKES ME FEEL BETTER.
TIME TO FINISH THE JOB.
I WATCH IT ALL COME DOWN. I WATCH IT ALL BURN; THE HOUSE I GREW UP IN, THE BAR I DRANK IN, THE PARK AND THE SCHOOL AND UNCLE MARTIN'S STORE.
MY LIFE GOES UP IN FLAMES.

EVERYTHING THAT WAS HUMAN IS GONE.
EXCEPT FOR ONE THING.

ONE MEMORY OF A PERFECT DAY REMAINS AS I STAND IN THE BLAZING RUINS.
THE MEMORY OF A SUNLIT SPRING DAY ON THE LAKE. THE DAY I ASKED WANDA TO MARRY ME.
BEST DAY OF MY LIFE.

I USE MY MIND TO COLLAPSE THE ENTIRE SCENE, SHAPING THE PSYCHOPLASM INTO A MORE MANAGEABLE FORM.

I TAKE THAT LAST MEMORY AND REDUCE IT DOWN TO A SINGLE SPARK.
THAT WAS THE BEST DAY, BEST THING I EVER DID. IT'S WORTH KEEPING BUT I'D ONLY BREAK IT OR LOSE IT.

GUESS I SHOULD PUT IT SOMEWHERE SAFE.

QUEENS, NEW YORK.
LOOK AT THAT RAIN!
YEAH, IT'S A HELL OF A NIGHT, WANDA.
ARE YOU OKAY? YOU SEEM KIND OF RESTLESS OR SOMETHING.
I DON'T KNOW. JUST THINKING...
WE'RE SO LUCKY, AREN'T WE, TERRY? WE'VE GOT EVERYTHING WE EVER WANTED.
I JUST FEEL SORRY FOR ANY POOR THING THAT HAS TO BE OUT THERE.
WANDA.
I SAVED IT FOR YOU.

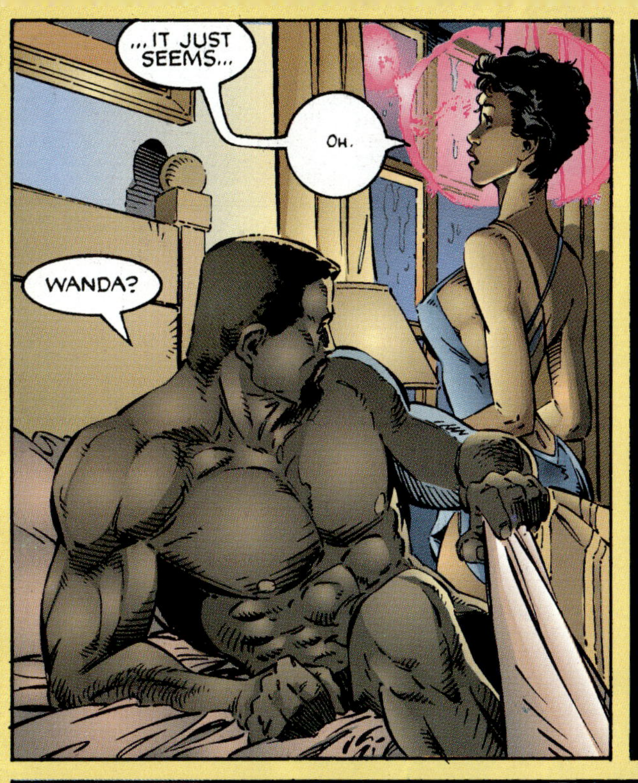
...IT JUST SEEMS...
OH.
WANDA?

I JUST... SOMETHING JUST CAME INTO MY HEAD. I SEEMED TO REMEMBER SOMETHING... AND THEN IT WAS GONE...
IT WAS...

I LOVE YOU.

CLOSE THE DRAPES, HONEY.
COME TO BED.
THE WINDOW GOES DARK.
THE WORLD GOES DARK.
BUT THAT'S OKAY. I'M USED TO IT.

DARKNESS IS MY HOME NOW.
1993

SPAWN
TM
image
19
OCT
$1.95
'2" Canada
S H O W T I M E
P a r t   O n e

SUNDAY
INDEPENDENT
LOS ANGELES
FIVE CENTS
NOVEMBER 5 1916
HOUDINI ASTOUNDS CAPACITY AU
DEFIES 10 HANDCUFFS & STRAITJ
CONCERNED POLICE ATTENTIVE

HOUDINI

A BUNKER UNDER NAGASAKI, JAPAN. AUGUST 9, 1945.

THE WAR IS NEARLY LOST. WITH ALL OTHER OPTIONS EXHAUSTED, THERE IS ONE TACTIC YET UNTRIED.

MEN OF INFLUENCE FROM RELIGION, BUSINESS AND THE MILITARY FOCUS THEIR ENERGIES TO GAIN AID FROM THE ARMY OF A DIFFERENT EMPEROR...

... ONE OF DARKNESS.

ELSEWHEN/WHERE...

QUICK! I THINK SOMETHING'S ABOUT TO COME THROUGH!

YOU'LL BE GLAD I FOUND THIS WINDOW, %^2!

"A PITY THERE WASN'T THE TIME TO SET UP ANY CONTROLS, OR SUFFICIENT MEASUREMENT SCHEMES. WE ARE FORTUNATE THAT YOU DISCOVERED THIS EVENT WINDOW AT ALL."
"NOW, THE BOMB, I AM GLAD THESE EARTHIANS FOUND A SECOND ONE NECESSARY."
"THIS ATOMIC EVENT MAY TELL US SOMETHING ABOUT THE EFFECTS OF MUNDANE HIGH-ENERGY PARTICLE BOMBARD-MENT ON INFERNAL MATTER. IT HAS ALREADY BEEN DETERMINED THAT NEITHER BLAST FORCE NOR HEAT CAN FAZE A HELL-CREATURE."
"WE'RE DEFINITELY REGISTERING INFERNAL MATTER, SIR-- IT'S UNMISTAKABLE!"
"THEY'VE DONE IT! THEY'VE BRIDGED THE ABYSS!"

I WAS RIGHT! WE'RE NO LONGER REGISTERING THE INFERNAL MATTER!

BUT WHERE DID THE HELL-CREATURE GO?

PERHAPS WE HAVE UNDERESTIMATED THE POTENCY OF THIS BLAST, AND ITS FEEDBACK TO OUR MONITORS. WHO COULD HAVE ANTICIPATED THAT THIS ENERGY RELEASE WOULD BE OF ANY SIGNIFICANCE TO US, ON OUR PLANAR LEVEL?

THIS MERITS FURTHER INVESTIGATION, BUT IT IS OF NO REAL URGENCY. %19, SEE TO IT.

SOMEWHERE IN THE SOVIET UNION, SEVERAL YEARS AGO...
"INHALE.
"HOLD IT."
"STEADY.
"CLOSER. THERE'S YOUSEF VOLOKHOV.
JUST SQUEEZE...
BUT INSTEAD...
...THERE'S NO TIME TO MAKE THE SHOT.
JEE-ZUS!
MOVE IT, SIMMONS!
SPAK
SPAK
SPAK
SPAK
SPAK
SPAK

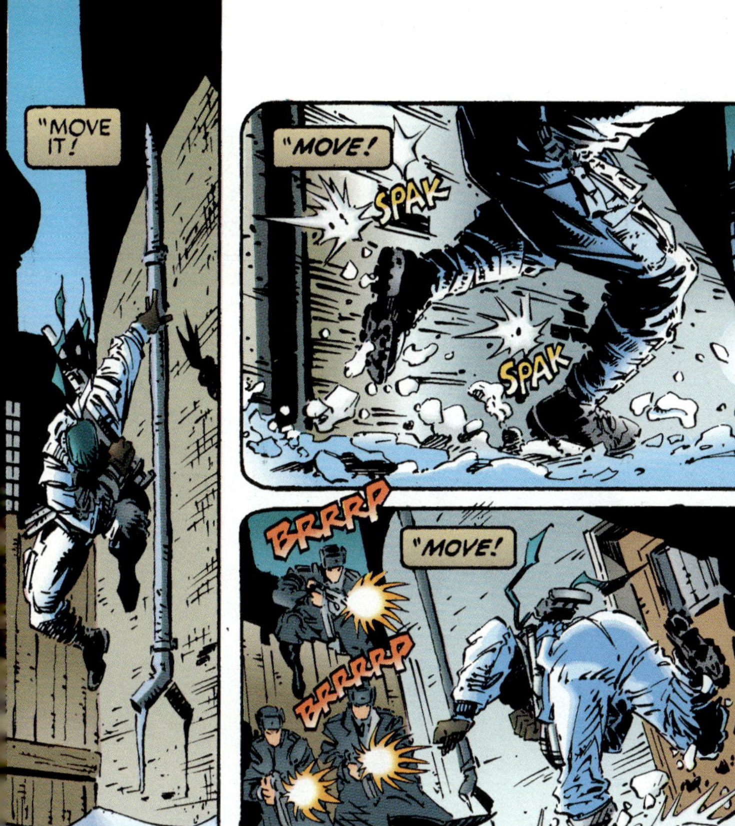
"MOVE IT!"
"MOVE!"
SPAK
SPAK
"MOVE!"
BRRRP
BRRRP

BRRRP
BRRRP
"MOVE!"
"MOVE!"
"MOVE!"

KRRCH!
"INSIDE! NOW!"

KLIK

THE BOWERY, NEW YORK CITY.
5:10 A.M.
SQUEE
SQUEE
SQUEE
KLIK

Ohhh... NIGHTMARE...
EH?
THAT WASN'T THERE WHEN I WENT TO SL--
BUH-TAAASSH!

RAARH!
BUT IT WAS JUST A PILE OF RAGS! BUMS DON'T DRESS IN THOSE COLORS!
GOD
GOD
GOD
GOD
GOD
GOD
TFOOP
YOU'RE MEAT!
ULGK!
WE NEED TO TALK, HELL'S-PAWN.
I CAN'T LET HIM GET AWAY! HE BLEW ME UP!
DON'T WORRY ABOUT IT. I SNARED HIS WALLET, AND WE CAN FIND HIM LATER. FOR NOW, WE HAVE MORE PRESSING MATTERS TO DISCUSS.

GRAB RANDOM PIECES FROM ALL OVER THE EARTH AND THROW THEM TOGETHER ON A SMALL ISLAND. THIS GIVES YOU MANHATTAN, AND MAKES IT THE GREATEST CITY IN THE WORLD.
THE BOWERY SLAPS AGAINST GREENWICH VILLAGE, WHICH BORDERS CHINATOWN AND LITTLE ITALY. HALF AN HOUR'S DRIVE UPTOWN ONE FINDS LITTLE UKRAINE, SANDWICHED BETWEEN CENTRAL PARK WEST AND HARLEM. SOME OF THE SHOPS THERE HAVE BILINGUAL SIGNS BECAUSE SOME OF THE LOCALS HAVE A BETTER GRASP OF CYRILLIC.
IT'S A PERFECT NEIGHBORHOOD. NEEDLESS TO SAY, THERE'S NO SHORTAGE OF GOSSIP.

TOPIC THIS EARLY MORNING: PORSCHE MacNEILL.
<HERE COMES THAT LAZY KID AGAIN.*>
<TWENTY-TWO YEARS OLD. BIG SHOT HAS HIS OWN APARTMENT DOWNTOWN, BUT STILL HE BRINGS HIS DIRTY SOCKS HOME TO MOMMA.>
<NO RESPECT FOR ANYONE, THAT KID.>
<WHEN I WAS HIS AGE, I STAYED AROUND AND SUPPORTED MY MOTHER AND FAMILY.>
*TRANSLATED FROM UKRANIAN.

<THAT'S WHAT HAPPENS, YOU MARRY OUT OF THE NEIGHBORHOOD. YOUR CHILDREN ARE BUMS.>
<FEH, THAT SCOT.>
<AT LEAST THE KID HAS A GOOD JOB, IN ELECTRONICS.>
<AND SPEAKING OF JOBS...>
<...I'D BETTER BE GETTING TO THE AIRPORT. AN OLD FRIEND CALLED TO SAY THAT HE'S COMING IN, AND HIS LUGGAGE NEEDS SPECIAL CARE.>

...AND IF YOU ASK ME, POLITICAL AND FINANCIAL ISSUES ASIDE, THESE GENTLE-MEN NEED SOME SERIOUS FASHION ADVICE. FIRST TIME TO TOWN, FARMBOYS? I THINK MY GRANDFATHER WAS BURIED IN ONE OF THOSE SUITS. I HAVE A WORD OF ENGLISH THEY SHOULD ALL TAKE THE TIME TO LEARN: ARMANI!
E!
ENTERTAINMENT TELEVISION

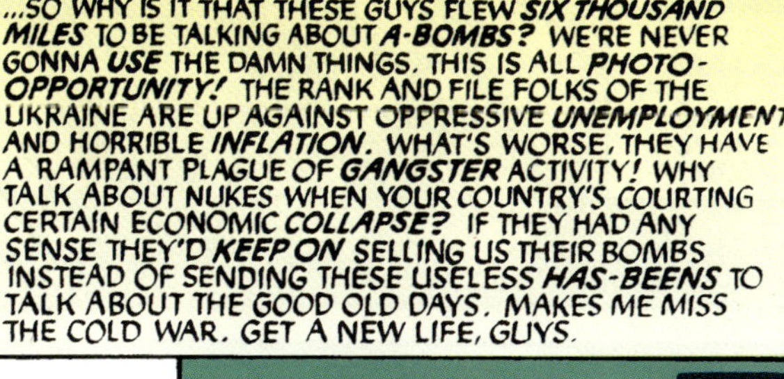
...FOR THE FIRST TIME EVER, NUCLEAR TECHNICIANS FROM THE FORMER SOVIET BLOC NATIONS WILL BE MEETING WITH THEIR GLOBAL COUNTERPARTS IN AN INFORMAL SETTING. THE THREE-DAY CONFERENCE, WHICH OPENS TOMORROW AT NEW YORK'S COLUMBIA UNIVERSITY, HAS BEEN HAILED AS YET ANOTHER SIGN THAT THE COLD WAR HAS ENDED.
CNN

...SO WHY IS IT THAT THESE GUYS FLEW SIX THOUSAND MILES TO BE TALKING ABOUT A-BOMBS? WE'RE NEVER GONNA USE THE DAMN THINGS. THIS IS ALL PHOTO-OPPORTUNITY! THE RANK AND FILE FOLKS OF THE UKRAINE ARE UP AGAINST OPPRESSIVE UNEMPLOYMENT AND HORRIBLE INFLATION. WHAT'S WORSE, THEY HAVE A RAMPANT PLAGUE OF GANGSTER ACTIVITY! WHY TALK ABOUT NUKES WHEN YOUR COUNTRY'S COURTING CERTAIN ECONOMIC COLLAPSE? IF THEY HAD ANY SENSE THEY'D KEEP ON SELLING US THEIR BOMBS INSTEAD OF SENDING THESE USELESS HAS-BEENS TO TALK ABOUT THE GOOD OLD DAYS. MAKES ME MISS THE COLD WAR. GET A NEW LIFE, GUYS.
5
TALKBACK

HAULING LUGGAGE. ALWAYS LUGGAGE. THIRTY-ONE YEARS AGO, ANDREI ZLENKO LEFT HIS UKRANIAN HOMELAND ON A TEMPORARY VISA, CARRYING WHAT LITTLE HE OWNED IN SHABBY SUITCASES. EVERY DAY, AT HIS JOB, HE IS REMINDED OF THAT EVENT. HE WONDERS IF HE WILL STILL BE CARRYING LUGGAGE IN THE AFTERLIFE.
AT THE TIME HE LEFT, HE'D HAD NO INTENTION OF RETURNING TO THE OLD COUNTRY. NOW, HE SOMETIMES FINDS HIMSELF LOOKING WHISTFULLY BACK ON THOSE SIMPLER DAYS...UNTIL HE REMEMBERS THE SECRET POLICE.

THAT MEMORY HAS BECOME MORE VIVID JUST NOW. HE RECOGNIZES THE CHEAP LUGGAGE, THE NAMES OF THE RUSSIAN CITIES ON THE TRAVEL STICKERS... AND THE WATCHFUL EYES. HIS OLD NEIGHBOR YOUSEF'S CONSPICUOUSLY STURDY CARRYING CASE SLIDES INTO VIEW.

THE UNIFORM OF HIS OVERSEER IS DIFFERENT, YET STILL A UNIFORM. DAMNED THUGS. A MAN CAN RISK ALL TO TRANSPORT HIMSELF TO THE OTHER SIDE OF THE WORLD...
... AND THE WORST OF THE OLD LIFE CAN FIND A WAY TO FOLLOW.

INSPECTED BY UNITED STATES CUSTOMS
NO MATTER. THE OVERSEER IS JUST A FORMALITY. YOUSEF IS AN OLD FRIEND, AND THAT FRIENDSHIP IS WORTH AT LEAST THIS SMALL FAVOR.

COLUMBIA UNIVERSITY. IT IS LATE ON A SATURDAY EVENING, THE SECOND DAY OF THE "EAST-WEST ATOMIC WARFARE, SCIENCE AND APPLICATIONS CONFERENCE."
SEVERAL SPEAKERS FROM THE EASTERN BLOC DECIDE TO SAMPLE THE REAL AMERICA-- ONE THAT DECADES OF SOVIET PROPOGANDA HAD BURNED INTO THEIR MINDS.
FAR FROM A WARNING, IT HAS BECOME A BEACON-- AN IDEAL.
<GENTLEMEN, WE HAVE ARRIVED.*>
<A TRULY MAGNIFICENT RESULT OF A FREE SOCIETY.>
<A TRULY MAGNIFICENT RESULT OF BREEDING, TOO.>
<LET US GO INSIDE AND DRINK.>
*TRANSLATED FROM RUSSIAN.
TAXI
XXX PEEP SHOWS 25¢
TOW AWAY ZONE
LIVE SEX SHOW
LIVE O HOOTE
<YOU KNOW, IT IS SUCH A SHAME THAT OUR SCIENCE WILL NEVER BE PUT TO PRACTICAL USE.>
<YES, OURS IS A DYING PROFESSION. WHAT GOOD IS IT TO KNOW HOW TO DESTROY THE EARTH, IF WE NEVER GET THE CHANCE?>
<I DON'T KNOW. PERHAPS THERE WILL YET BE A USE FOR OUR KNOWLEDGE. CHEER UP!>

SEVERAL ROUNDS LATER...
‹ANY SPY WORTH HIS METTLE WOULD LOVE OUR FUSION DATA. JUST TODAY I WAS SPEAKING WITH A COLLEAGUE FROM ISRAEL...›
‹THEIR BOMBS ARE QUITE EFFICIENT. A SHAME THAT THEY MUST KEEP IT SECRET.›
‹I STILL PREFER THE OLD, TRIED AND TRUE ATOMICS. THEY'RE SO EASY TO JUST DISMANTLE, PICK UP AND TAKE ANYWHERE WITH YOU.›
‹DID ANY OF YOU MEET KHADAFY'S ENVOY? NOW THERE IS A MAN COULD MAKE US ALL VERY WEALTHY, I BET!›

PHONE
‹THIS IS MISHA. GET ME STATION CHIEF IVANOV. NOW.›

‹OH MAMA!›
‹YOU WERE RIGHT. LOUD, CRAZY TALK GOT ONE OF OUR KGB SHADOWS OUT OF THE WAY, AND NOW THE OTHER'S DISTRACTED.›
‹LET'S HEAD FOR THE EXIT!›

‹IDIOT! I LEAVE FOR A MOMENT AND THEY SLIP AWAY!›
‹I'LL TRY TO NAB THEM! YOU CALL IT IN, THIS TIME!›
EXIT

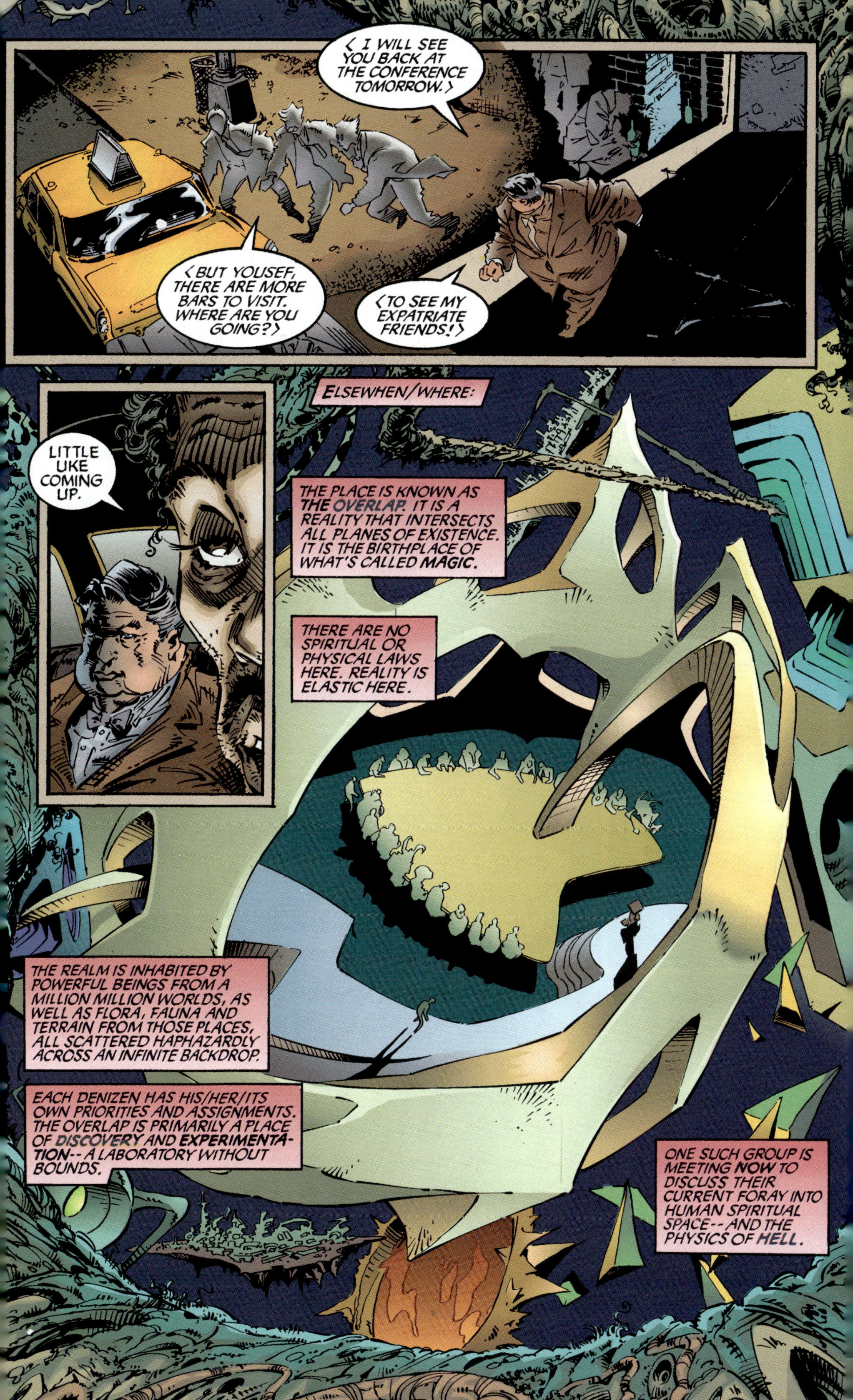
I WILL SEE YOU BACK AT THE CONFERENCE TOMORROW.
BUT YOUSEF, THERE ARE MORE BARS TO VISIT. WHERE ARE YOU GOING?
TO SEE MY EXPATRIATE FRIENDS!
LITTLE UKE COMING UP.
ELSEWHEN/WHERE:
THE PLACE IS KNOWN AS THE OVERLAP. IT IS A REALITY THAT INTERSECTS ALL PLANES OF EXISTENCE. IT IS THE BIRTHPLACE OF WHAT'S CALLED MAGIC.
THERE ARE NO SPIRITUAL OR PHYSICAL LAWS HERE. REALITY IS ELASTIC HERE.
THE REALM IS INHABITED BY POWERFUL BEINGS FROM A MILLION MILLION WORLDS, AS WELL AS FLORA, FAUNA AND TERRAIN FROM THOSE PLACES, ALL SCATTERED HAPHAZARDLY ACROSS AN INFINITE BACKDROP.
EACH DENIZEN HAS HIS/HER/ITS OWN PRIORITIES AND ASSIGNMENTS. THE OVERLAP IS PRIMARILY A PLACE OF DISCOVERY AND EXPERIMENTA-TION-- A LABORATORY WITHOUT BOUNDS.
ONE SUCH GROUP IS MEETING NOW TO DISCUSS THEIR CURRENT FORAY INTO HUMAN SPIRITUAL SPACE-- AND THE PHYSICS OF HELL.

THANKS FOR COMING. I COULDN'T BE MORE EXCITED, NOW THAT THINGS ARE MOVING!
I'VE BEEN KEEPING AN EYE ON THOSE EARTHIANS AND THEIR ATOMIC FETISH-- AND THEY HAVEN'T ALL KILLED EACH OTHER YET! SO, I'VE MANAGED TO PUSH THINGS IN A DIRECTION THAT'LL GIVE US SOME ANSWERS SOON.
OUR LAST SURVEY-- WHERE A HELL-CREATURE WAS BLOWN UP-- WAS A BUST, BUT THAT'S OKAY. WE WEREN'T PREPARED FOR THAT EVENT THE WAY WE ARE NOW.
THIS TIME, I PLUGGED A THOUGHT-PROGRAM INTO A SCIENTIST THERE. HE'LL DETONATE AN ATOM BOMB AT A PRE-SET TIME. A DEMON, THE LATEST HELL'S-PAWN WILL BE NEAR GROUND ZERO.
WE'VE PLACED AN AGENT THERE WHO'LL MAKE SURE THAT THE CREATURE'S IN PLACE. WE KNOW THE STRENGTH OF THE BLAST, SO WE'VE TAKEN VIEWING PRECAUTIONS.
SO NOW-- OUR CONCLUSIVE TEST TO DETERMINE IF ATOMICS CAN KILL DEMONS, AND IN THE PROCESS SCATTER THEIR INFERNAL MATTER!
AND THE BEST PART IS, THAT PERSNICKETY PEST HOUDINI IS THE AGENT ON THE SCENE! WE CLEAR UP TWO PROBLEMS AT ONCE!
AM I GOOD, OR WHAT?
I TRUST THAT THE PEST WILL VERIFY THE NATURE OF THE HELL-CREATURE'S POWERS AND TEMPERMENT FIRST. THAT WILL BE USEFUL INFORMATION SHOULD WE DECIDE TO WORK ON HELL IN THE FUTURE. THE PLACE IS RIPE FOR MANIPULATION.
HOUDINI IS USING ONE OF OUR PORTAL DEVICES. I TOLD HIM IT IS MORE EFFICIENT A TRANSPORT THAN MEDITATION, OR WHATEVER HIS USUAL METHOD. IN HIS CONFUSION OVER THE FAILURE OF OUR DEVICE, HE WILL NOT HAVE TIME TO ADJUST TO HIS NORMAL MODE OF TRANSFER, AND WILL PERISH.
BRILLIANT!
Hmm... BUT HE ALWAYS ESCAPES...

LITTLE UKRAINE, TOWARD MIDNIGHT.

EXCUSE ME, PLEASE... ANDREI ZLENKO IS...?

Huh?

I LOOK FOR ANDREI ZLENKO.

OK, YEAH. TRY 301. BUT IT'S PAST THE OLD MAN'S BEDTIME, I THINK.

NO MANNERS.

SONY

GREENWICH VILLAGE, HALF AN HOUR LATER...

RADIO HUT

IBM APPLE

40% OFF POWER PC

I GOTTA GET OUTTA THIS RUT. MY LIFE, IN THREE WORDS, WOULD BE: BORING. UNDER-TASKED. ASSISTANT MANAGER.

MAKE THAT FOUR WORDS.

LUU-CY! I'M HO-OME!

FOR ONCE, IT'S A GOOD THING THE CLEANING SERVICE IS ON STRIKE.

EMPLOYEES ONLY

SONY

...SO CHECK THIS OUT: LAST NIGHT I SET OFF ANOTHER ONE OF MY BEAUTS, BUT SOME DUDE CHASED ME. HE WAS ALL ON FIRE AN' SCREAMIN'! IT WAS COOL!

I BET YOU WET YOUR PANTS, BUDDY.

NOT EVEN! BUT WHATEVER IT TAKES, I'LL GET RID OF THOSE BUMS BY MY PLACE.

WHAT ABOUT THE BUMS BY YOUR MA'S PLACE? THAT'S WHERE YOU HANG OUT ALL THE TIME!

BITE ME. ANYWAY, I GOTTA GET BACK TO WORK HERE. THIS NEXT ONE IS GONNA BE BRIGHT.

THERE'S NO WAY I'M GOING TO BELIEVE YOU'RE HARRY HOUDINI.

WELL... YOU'RE A DEMON FROM HELL...!

AREN'T YOU DEAD OR SOMETHING?

AREN'T YOU?

I GET YOUR POINT. BUT THIS IS PRETTY HARD TO BELIEVE...

WHICH PART? THAT I'M A DIMENSION-TRAVELLING HYPER-MAGE TEN THOUSAND TIMES MORE POWERFUL THAN MY STAGE ACT LET ON, OR THAT YOU'RE AN INVULNER-ABLE, ULTRASTRONG, HORRIBLE PUPPET OF HELL?

BOTH, I GUESS.

HOWEVER, I DIDN'T COME HERE TO DISCUSS OUR MUTUALLY UNBELIEVABLE CONDITIONS... I'M HERE TO SPEAK ABOUT YOU, HELL'S-PAWN... AND ABOUT YOUR POWERS.

WHAT DO YOU KNOW ABOUT MY POWERS? YOU'RE JUST AN ESCAPE ARTIST.

JUST AN ESCAPE ARTIST? JUST AN ESCAPE ARTIST?! ARE YOU AWARE OF HOW MANY YEARS I'VE SPENT, NON-MAGICAL, GRUELING YEARS, LEARNING TO BE JUST AN ESCAPE ARTIST?!

GOOD-- I'VE TWEAKED HIS CURIOSITY.

AS IT TURNED OUT, THOSE LEVELS OF CONCENTRATION LED TO MY ACCIDENTAL EXTRA-DIMENSIONAL DISCOVERIES... THINGS BE-YOND HOCUS-POCUS AND MERE SPIRITUALISM.

NOW I KNOW MAGIC. REAL MAGIC.

foop

SO WHAT DID YOU SEE? AN ILLUSION? A SMOKE PELLET? TELEPOR-TATION?

DOES IT MATTER?

THAT WAS MAGIC-- THAT I MOVED FROM POINT "A" TO POINT "B" IN A NON-MUNDANE MANNER. IT WAS THE RESULT, NOT THE METHOD THAT MATTERED.

MAGIC IS ABOUT PERCEPTION AND THE WILL'S ABILITY TO ALTER THAT PERCEPTION, USING ENERGIES GATHERED FROM BEYOND THIS WORLD.
MAGIC IS LIKE TELLING A LIE SO CONVINCING THAT EVEN THE UNIVERSE BELIEVES YOU! AND YOU, MY FRIEND, ARE A CREATURE OF MAGIC, ALBEIT OF FINITE POWER. HOWEVER, YOU NEEDN'T EXHAUST YOUR POWER...
...THAT SYMBIOTIC COSTUME CAN DO MUCH OF YOUR WORK FOR YOU.
GOOD GOD! QUICK-- BEHIND YOU!
KLSSSKKKKK
YOU SEE? WITH ONLY A THOUGHT, YOUR SUIT ATTACKS FOR YOU. IT EXPENDS ITS ENERGY, NOT YOURS.
SKRAK!
NOW, IN THE CASE OF THIS BOMB...
...THE SUIT APPRECIATED THE THREAT AND ACTED TO KEEP YOU FROM HARM, WITHOUT YOUR CONSCIOUS DIRECTION. YOUR ENERGY EXPENDITURE? NONE.
AND THERE'S MORE.

YOUR MOST IMPORTANT POWER, AS A CREATURE OF SORCERY, IS MANIFESTATION. WITH A CLEAR HEAD AND A STRONG WILL YOU CAN CAUSE YOUR COSTUME TO MAKE JUST ABOUT ANYTHING, PROVIDED YOU UNDERSTAND ITS ESSENCE...
...ITS SIZE, THE WEIGHT, THE COLOR-- THAT SORT OF THING.
FOR EXAMPLE, THINK OF SOMETHING SMALL, LIKE A MARBLE.
YOU KNOW WHAT IT FEELS LIKE, LOOKS LIKE AND ALL. NOW FEEL YOUR DESIRE FOR SUCCESS FADE TO SURENESS. YOU WILL SUCCEED. LET THIS WILLPOWER ACTIVATE YOUR COSTUME. REACH OUT... THE MOLECULES ARE FLOATING FREE...GRAB THEM...THINK MARBLE ...GO ON...
...MAKE ONE!
A MARBLE...
OKAY...
SHOOP
LOOKIE HERE, FELLAS! WE GOTS US A REG-U-LAR CIRCUS ON OUR ROOF!
PRETTY CLOSE... WE'LL TRY AGAIN...
BRAINS, DIVVY... YOU AN' ME, WE TAKE THE RICH GUY IN THE TUX. LINK, TAKE THE GEEK.
YEAH... heh heh... YOU SAID IT, SMOKEY!
YEAH... heh heh. COME AN' GET ME.

KLOK
LINK? Oh, PUH-LEEZ.
LINK, MEET CHAIN.
CHAIN... LINK.
WHUFF
GOOMPH
BRAINS... DIVVY... SMOKEY...? LET YOUR NAMES SPEAK YOUR FATE.
AAAAAA!
...
PUTTZZZ
HUHNHH...

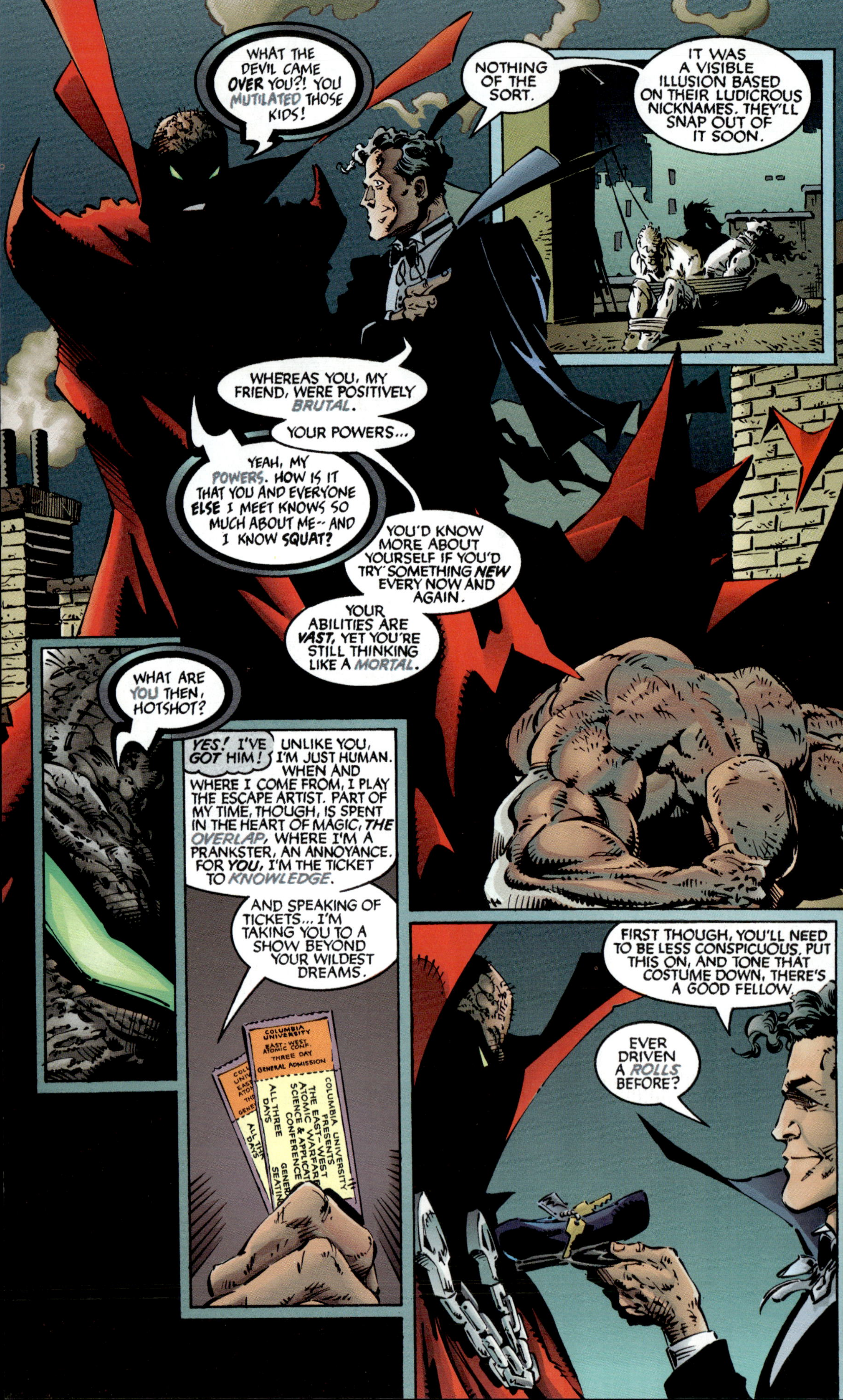

WHAT THE DEVIL CAME OVER YOU?! YOU MUTILATED THOSE KIDS!
NOTHING OF THE SORT.
IT WAS A VISIBLE ILLUSION BASED ON THEIR LUDICROUS NICKNAMES. THEY'LL SNAP OUT OF IT SOON.
WHEREAS YOU, MY FRIEND, WERE POSITIVELY BRUTAL.
YOUR POWERS...
YEAH, MY POWERS. HOW IS IT THAT YOU AND EVERYONE ELSE I MEET KNOWS SO MUCH ABOUT ME-- AND I KNOW SQUAT?
YOU'D KNOW MORE ABOUT YOURSELF IF YOU'D TRY SOMETHING NEW EVERY NOW AND AGAIN.
YOUR ABILITIES ARE VAST, YET YOU'RE STILL THINKING LIKE A MORTAL.
WHAT ARE YOU THEN, HOTSHOT?
YES! I'VE GOT HIM!
UNLIKE YOU, I'M JUST HUMAN. WHEN AND WHERE I COME FROM, I PLAY THE ESCAPE ARTIST. PART OF MY TIME, THOUGH, IS SPENT IN THE HEART OF MAGIC, THE OVERLAP, WHERE I'M A PRANKSTER, AN ANNOYANCE. FOR YOU, I'M THE TICKET TO KNOWLEDGE.
AND SPEAKING OF TICKETS... I'M TAKING YOU TO A SHOW BEYOND YOUR WILDEST DREAMS.
COLUMBIA UNIVERSITY
EAST-WEST ATOMIC CONF.
THREE DAY
GENERAL ADMISSION
COLUMBIA UNIVERSITY PRESENTS THE EAST-WEST ATOMIC WARFARE SCIENCE & APPLICATIONS CONFERENCE
ALL THREE DAYS
GENERAL SEATING
FIRST THOUGH, YOU'LL NEED TO BE LESS CONSPICUOUS, PUT THIS ON, AND TONE THAT COSTUME DOWN, THERE'S A GOOD FELLOW.
EVER DRIVEN A ROLLS BEFORE?

AT THAT MOMENT, THREE STORIES BELOW...
...SPLATTER 'EM ALL WITH PAINT...
...WHY DON'T THOSE CREEPS JUST TAKE THE HINT AND LEAVE?
STICK AROUND, MY BOY, AND SOON YOU'LL BE ABLE TO DO THIS WITH A FLICK OF THE WRIST--
AND THEN, BELOW...
IT'S THAT DAMN KID AGAIN!
ANNOYING WHELP.
THIS TIME, HE'S TOAST!
I'M GONNA NAIL THAT PUNK TO THE WALL WITH HIS OWN BONES!
I'M GONNA... I'M GONNA ...!
DRIVE.
RIGHT BEHIND YOU, HELL'S-PAWN.

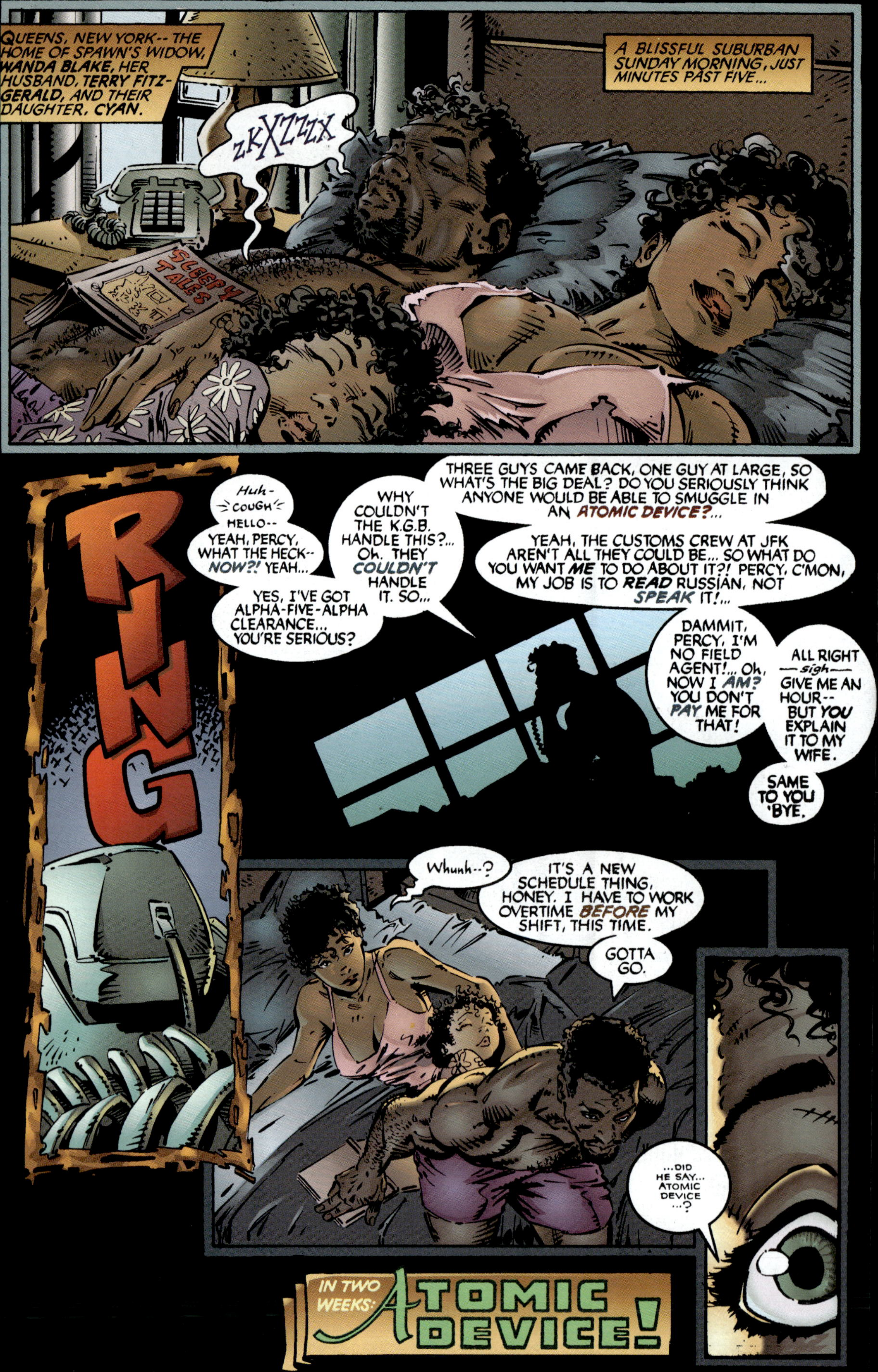

QUEENS, NEW YORK-- THE HOME OF SPAWN'S WIDOW, WANDA BLAKE, HER HUSBAND, TERRY FITZGERALD, AND THEIR DAUGHTER, CYAN.
A BLISSFUL SUBURBAN SUNDAY MORNING, JUST MINUTES PAST FIVE...
zKXZZZx
SLEEPY TALES
RING
Huh-- cough HELLO-- YEAH, PERCY, WHAT THE HECK-- NOW?! YEAH...
YES, I'VE GOT ALPHA-FIVE-ALPHA CLEARANCE... YOU'RE SERIOUS?
WHY COULDN'T THE K.G.B. HANDLE THIS?... Oh. THEY COULDN'T HANDLE IT. SO...
THREE GUYS CAME BACK, ONE GUY AT LARGE, SO WHAT'S THE BIG DEAL? DO YOU SERIOUSLY THINK ANYONE WOULD BE ABLE TO SMUGGLE IN AN ATOMIC DEVICE?...
YEAH, THE CUSTOMS CREW AT JFK AREN'T ALL THEY COULD BE... SO WHAT DO YOU WANT ME TO DO ABOUT IT?! PERCY, C'MON, MY JOB IS TO READ RUSSIAN, NOT SPEAK IT!...
DAMMIT, PERCY, I'M NO FIELD AGENT!... Oh, NOW I AM? YOU DON'T PAY ME FOR THAT!
ALL RIGHT -- sigh-- GIVE ME AN HOUR-- BUT YOU EXPLAIN IT TO MY WIFE.
SAME TO YOU 'BYE,
Whunh--?
IT'S A NEW SCHEDULE THING, HONEY. I HAVE TO WORK OVERTIME BEFORE MY SHIFT, THIS TIME.
GOTTA GO.
...DID HE SAY... ATOMIC DEVICE...?
IN TWO WEEKS: ATOMIC DEVICE!

SPAWN
image
20
NOV
$1.95
$3.75
CANADA

S H O W T I M E
P a r t   T w o

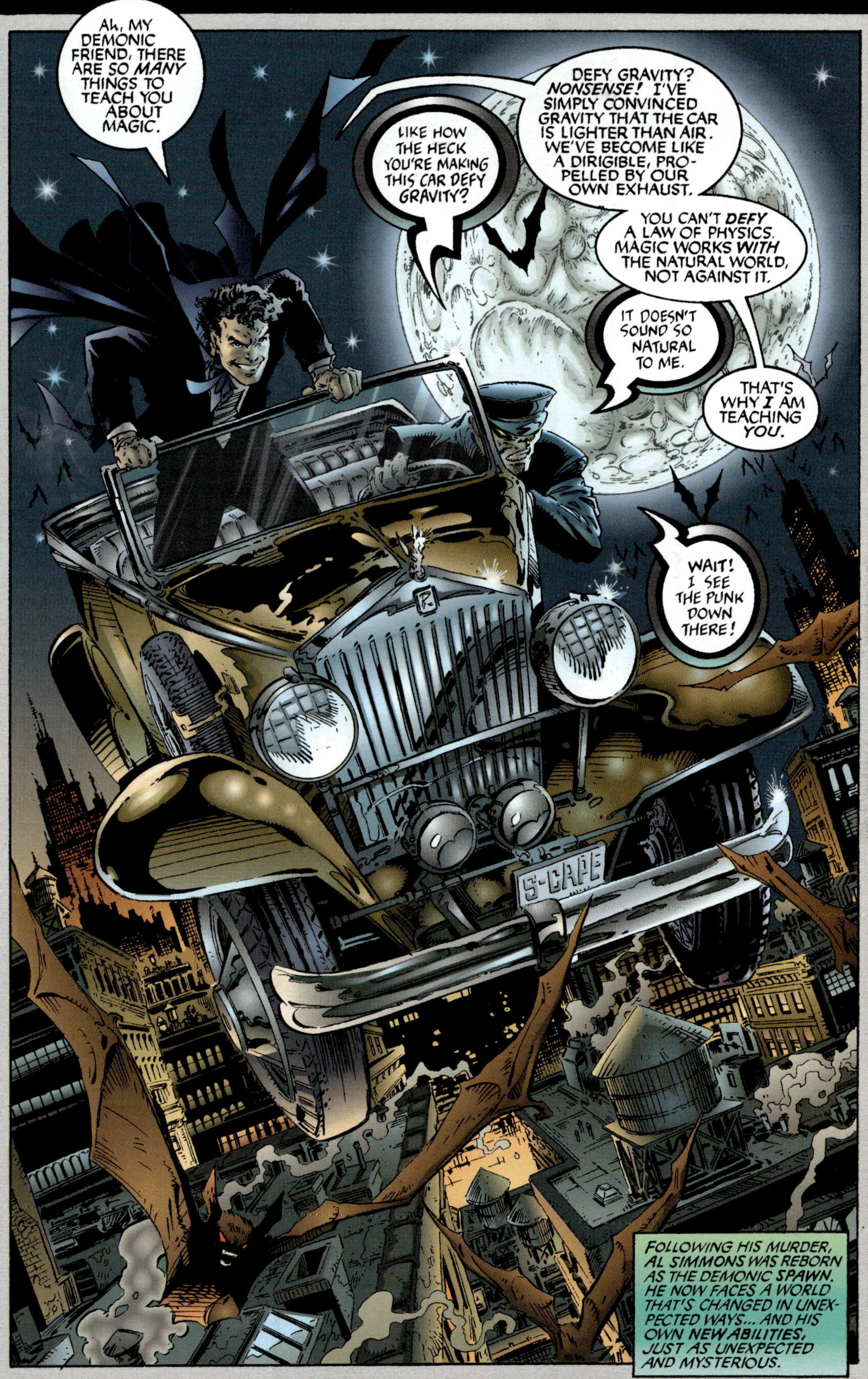

AH, MY DEMONIC FRIEND, THERE ARE SO MANY THINGS TO TEACH YOU ABOUT MAGIC.
LIKE HOW THE HECK YOU'RE MAKING THIS CAR DEFY GRAVITY?
DEFY GRAVITY? NONSENSE! I'VE SIMPLY CONVINCED GRAVITY THAT THE CAR IS LIGHTER THAN AIR. WE'VE BECOME LIKE A DIRIGIBLE, PROPELLED BY OUR OWN EXHAUST.
YOU CAN'T DEFY A LAW OF PHYSICS. MAGIC WORKS WITH THE NATURAL WORLD, NOT AGAINST IT.
IT DOESN'T SOUND SO NATURAL TO ME.
THAT'S WHY I AM TEACHING YOU.
WAIT! I SEE THE PUNK DOWN THERE!
S-CAPE
FOLLOWING HIS MURDER, AL SIMMONS WAS REBORN AS THE DEMONIC SPAWN. HE NOW FACES A WORLD THAT'S CHANGED IN UNEXPECTED WAYS... AND HIS OWN NEW ABILITIES, JUST AS UNEXPECTED AND MYSTERIOUS.

THE LATE NIGHT SILENCE OF MANHATTAN'S LITTLE UKRAINE IS CUT BY THE ROAR OF THE BOMBER'S SPEEDING CAR.
UNKNOWN TO HIM, A DEMON AND HIS NEW-FOUND MENTOR ARE IN SILENT PURSUIT.
I WONDER WHO HE'S MEETING HERE.
MAN, THAT WAS THE BEST ONE YET!
GOTTA CATCH THE NEWS-- SEE IF I MADE IT THIS TIME!
BISTR
HE'S GOTTA BE WORKING FOR THE MOB OR SOMEONE.
WHO CARES? WE CAN GET HIM LATER.
I'VE GOT TWO INVITES TO THE MAGICIANS' CLUB FOR SOME AFTER-HOURS FUN. ONE OF THEIR BOYS HAS A TRUNK OF MINE I'D LIKE TO LOOK IN ON. COMING?
THE HECK WITH THAT! I'M STICKING TO THIS KID LIKE GLUE!
SOMETHING'LL TURN UP.
SUIT YOURSELF. I'LL SEE YOU IN A FEW HOURS.
TIME PASSES SLOWLY... BUT WHEN HE WAS ALIVE AND A SOLDIER, AL SIMMONS WAS USED TO WAITING.

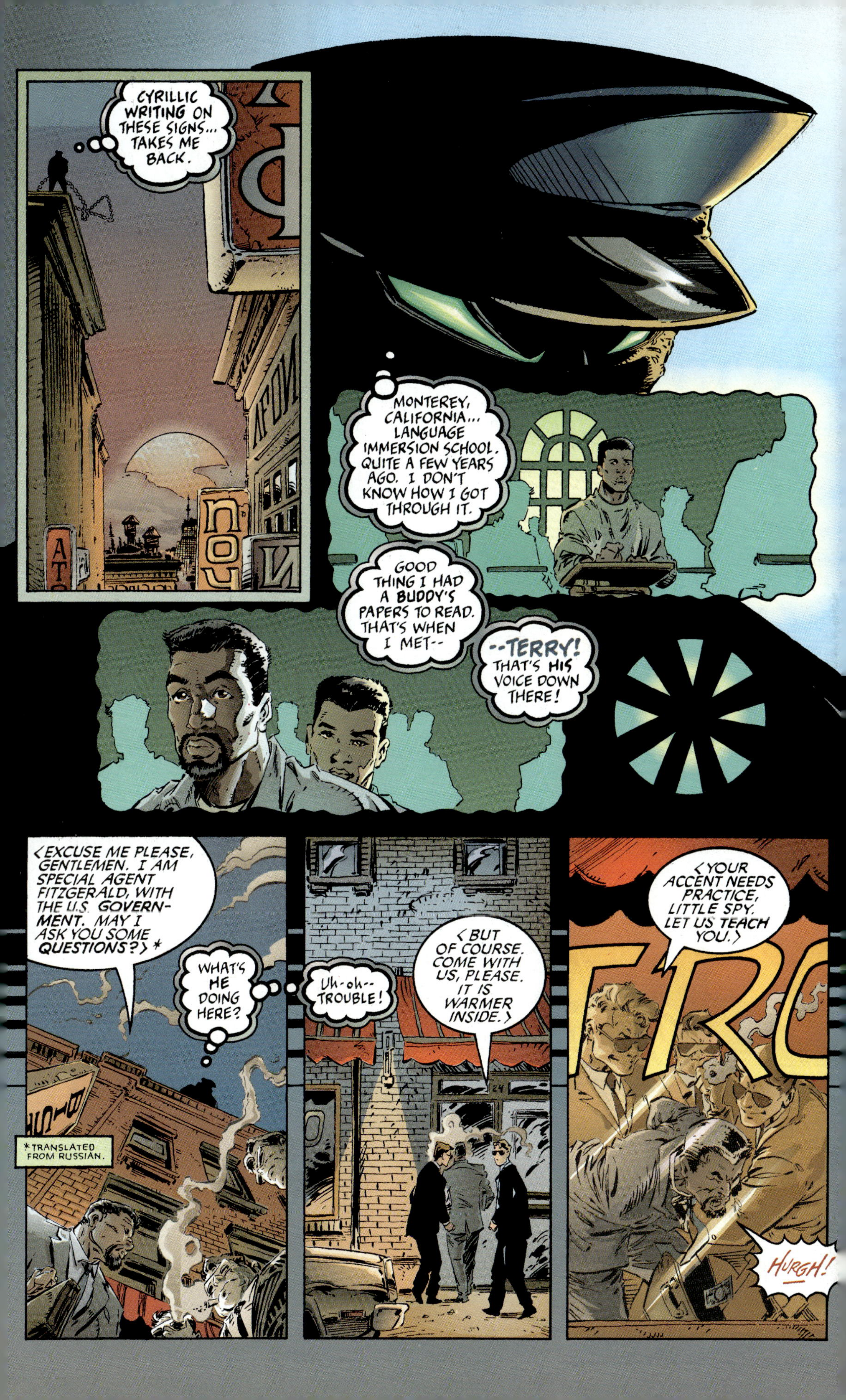

CYRILLIC WRITING ON THESE SIGNS... TAKES ME BACK.
MONTEREY, CALIFORNIA... LANGUAGE IMMERSION SCHOOL. QUITE A FEW YEARS AGO. I DON'T KNOW HOW I GOT THROUGH IT.
GOOD THING I HAD A BUDDY'S PAPERS TO READ. THAT'S WHEN I MET--
--TERRY! THAT'S HIS VOICE DOWN THERE!

<EXCUSE ME PLEASE, GENTLEMEN. I AM SPECIAL AGENT FITZGERALD, WITH THE U.S. GOVERNMENT. MAY I ASK YOU SOME QUESTIONS?> *
WHAT'S HE DOING HERE?
* TRANSLATED FROM RUSSIAN.
<BUT OF COURSE. COME WITH US, PLEASE. IT IS WARMER INSIDE.>
Uh-oh-- TROUBLE!

<YOUR ACCENT NEEDS PRACTICE, LITTLE SPY. LET US TEACH YOU.>
HURGH!

SKAATSSHH
LEAVE HIM ALONE!
KLOK!
THAT'S MY FRIEND!
SPT SPT SPT SPT SPT
ULP!
KLNK NK NK

IF IT WOULD HURT YOU MORE, I'D KILL YOU!
C'MON, TERRY, LET'S GO. WHAT'S THIS SAY... YOUSEF VOLOKHOV... JEEZ! I ALMOST BAGGED HIM YEARS AGO!
WHAT'S HE GOT TO DO WITH THIS MESS?
SAYS HE'S HERE FOR SOME WEAPONS CONFERENCE AND WENT AWOL. BUT WHERE--
SPLAK!

GO EASY THERE, TERRY. LEAN ON THIS CAR.
WHAAAT?? THAT'S VOLOKHOV IN FRONT OF THE PUNK'S BUILDING, OR I'M NOT DEAD!! I KNEW THIS THING STANK, BUT NOT THIS BAD!
DAVE'S PUB
NNNGGGHHH...

WHATEVER IT IS, THIS AGENT HAS GOT AN UNFINISHED DUTY TO EXECUTE!

...RUMOR HAS IT THAT OUR VISITING EASTERN EUROPEAN DIGNITARIES DID SOME DECIDEDLY UNDIGNIFIED CAROUSING LAST NIGHT, AND SHOWED UP AT ALL THE WRONG PARTIES. NEED A BROMO, COMRADES? SEEMS ONE OF YOUR PALS IS STILL OUT SLEEPING IT OFF.
ENTERTAINMENT TELEVISION
ungh
WHAT HIT ME? WHAT WAS UP WITH THOSE GUYS?
CAN'T LET TERRY KNOW WHO I AM...NOT YET.
...YOUSEF VOLOKHOV, A VISITING SCIENTIST FROM THE EAST-WEST ATOMIC WARFARE, SCIENCE AND APPLICATIONS CONFERENCE, IS STILL UNACCOUNTED FOR. SOURCES CLOSE TO THE NYPD HAVE INFORMED US OF A MAJOR SEARCH FOR THE MISSING TECHNICIAN. FOUL PLAY HAS NOT BEEN RULED OUT.
CNN
Y'KNOW, BROTHER, YOU MIGHT WANT TO BE MORE CAREFUL WITH THE PEOPLE AROUND HERE.
I GUESS YOU'RE RIGHT. THANKS, MISTER, FOR PULLIN' MY SKILLET OUT OF THE FIRE.
I'LL NEVER LET WANDA BECOME A WIDOW AGAIN.
IF YOU ASK ME, IT'S ALL ABOUT MONEY. THE RUSSIANS HAVE ALL THE ROMANCE AND LIMELIGHT OF BIG CHANGES. WHAT GETS LOST IN THE SHUFFLE IS THAT THE OTHER EX-SOVIET REPUBLICS ARE ALSO STRUGGLING FOR A NEW SYSTEM. THEY NEED MONEY, TOO! THE UKRAINE, WHERE VOLOKHOV IS FROM, COULD USE EVEN A FIFTH OF THE AID THAT HAS BEEN PROMISED TO RUSSIA.
PERCIVAL ISSACSEN-SMYTHE, PLEASE...
FITZGERALD, TERENCE D., A5A-923777...
YO, PERCY. I JUST GOT THE BEJEESUS KICKED OUT OF ME. NAH, SOME MATCH-CRISP DUDE HELPED ME OUT.
...NO, NO, WHAT I NEED IS FOR YOU TO ROLL ME DOWN SOME MUSCLE, STAT. THAT'S RIGHT, YOU BIT OFF MORE THAN I CAN CHEW!

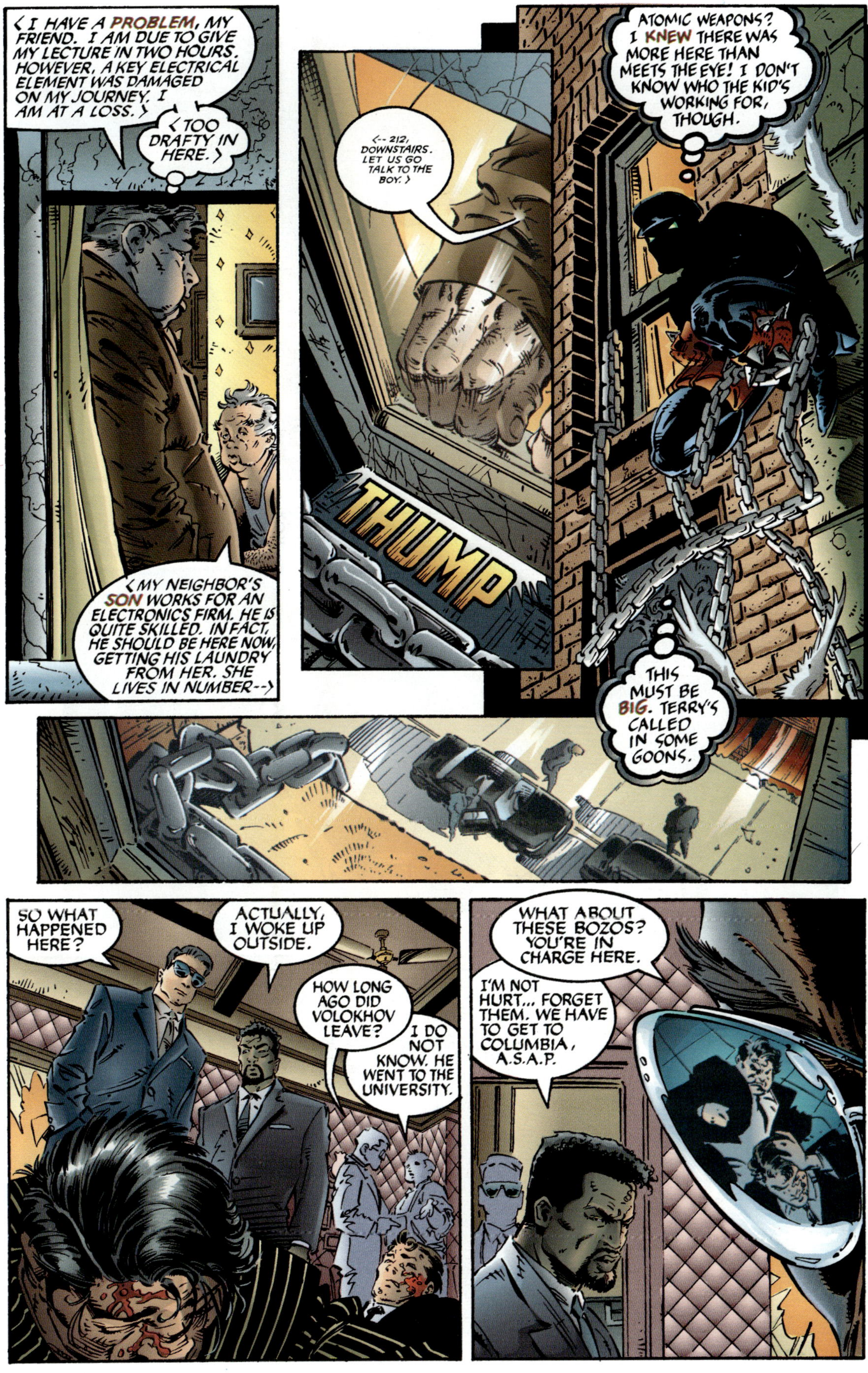

< I HAVE A PROBLEM, MY FRIEND. I AM DUE TO GIVE MY LECTURE IN TWO HOURS. HOWEVER, A KEY ELECTRICAL ELEMENT WAS DAMAGED ON MY JOURNEY. I AM AT A LOSS. >
< TOO DRAFTY IN HERE. >
< MY NEIGHBOR'S SON WORKS FOR AN ELECTRONICS FIRM. HE IS QUITE SKILLED. IN FACT, HE SHOULD BE HERE NOW, GETTING HIS LAUNDRY FROM HER. SHE LIVES IN NUMBER-- >
< -- 212, DOWNSTAIRS. LET US GO TALK TO THE BOY. >
THUMP
ATOMIC WEAPONS? I KNEW THERE WAS MORE HERE THAN MEETS THE EYE! I DON'T KNOW WHO THE KID'S WORKING FOR, THOUGH.
THIS MUST BE BIG. TERRY'S CALLED IN SOME GOONS.

SO WHAT HAPPENED HERE?
ACTUALLY, I WOKE UP OUTSIDE.
HOW LONG AGO DID VOLOKHOV LEAVE?
I DO NOT KNOW. HE WENT TO THE UNIVERSITY.

WHAT ABOUT THESE BOZOS? YOU'RE IN CHARGE HERE.
I'M NOT HURT... FORGET THEM. WE HAVE TO GET TO COLUMBIA, A.S.A.P.

YOU MISSED A GOOD SHOW, BUT NOTHING LIKE THE ONE WE'RE GOING TO NOW.
HOP IN!
BUT WE HAVE TO GET TO COLUMBIA UNIVERSITY! SOMETHING DANGEROUS IS GOING ON!
YOU PEEKED AT THESE, DIDN'T YOU? I GOT THEM FROM THE KID'S WALLET-- FRONT ROW, CENTER!
COLUMBIA UNIVERSITY... DAY THREE OF THE CONFERENCE.
I KNEW IT! THE KID WORKS FOR THE COMMIES!
WHAT EXACTLY IS VOLOKHOV GOING TO BE SPEAKING ABOUT?
DEMONSTRATION OF AN ATOMIC DETONATOR.
WE HAVE TO GET IN THERE. WE'RE WITH THE GOVERNMENT...
...F.B.I....
...N.R.C....
...uh, SECRET SERVICE...
NOT TO DIGRESS, GENTLEMEN, BUT IF YOU'RE NOT FACULTY, THAT'LL BE SIX BUCKS EACH.
WAIT A MINUTE... WHAT DOES HE MEAN, "DEMONSTRATION OF AN ATOMIC DETONATOR"?

GREENWICH VILLAGE...
RADIO H
PPLE

< AEROFLOT HAS FLOWN ME TO HEAVEN! >
IT'S A SCIENTIST'S SUPERMARKET! SONY! HITACHI! NEC !
CKARD BELL
YOU AMERICANS LEAD THE WORLD IN TECHNOLOGY!

ARE YOU SURE YOU CAN FIX MY DETONATOR IN TIME?
LOOK, OLD MAN, I'VE BUILT MORE DETONATORS THAN YOU'VE GOT CHINS...
EH?
EMPLOYEES ONLY
FRAGILE
ANDLE WITH CARE
FRAGILE
IBM
PS4 486DX 50
I SAID, NO PROBLEM. I'M ALMOST THERE.
I THINK?

GOOD, FOR WE MUST HURRY. WE ARE NEARLY LATE FOR MY LECTURE.
YAMAHA!
sigh

COLUMBIA UNIVERSITY, HALFWAY ACROSS TOWN AND LESS THAN AN HOUR LATER...

IT IS A SURPRISINGLY LARGE TURN-OUT FOR THE DRY TOPIC AT HAND. ONLY THE CONFERENCE PARTICIPANTS OR DEVOUT WEAPONRY WONKS WOULD BE INTERESTED IN FINELY ENGINEERED ATOMIC DETONATORS.
THEY WON'T BE DISAPPOINTED.
THE AUDIENCE GROWS QUIET AS YOUSEF VOLOKHOV, A PIONEER OF THE FORMER SOVIET UNION'S ATOMIC PROGRAM, WALKS TO THE PODIUM.
THIS IS HIS PROUDEST MOMENT. HE HAS SPENT OVER FORTY YEARS IN TOP-SECRET RESEARCH. NOW, AT LAST, HE CAN GAIN THE EYES AND EARS OF THE WORLD.
BUT THERE IS ANOTHER REASON FOR YOUSEF TO BE HERE. HIS OBJECTIVE IS NOT RECOGNITION. THE WELL-BEING OF HIS COUNTRY, THE UKRAINE, IS HIS SOLE CONCERN.
HE WITHDRAWS A SHIELDED CONTAINER.
THE MOMENT IS AT HAND. MEMBERS OF THE AUDIENCE SMILE IN RECOGNITION. THERE'S NO MISTAKING THE CHROMIUM STEEL OBJECT FOR ANYTHING BUT WHAT IT IS:
...AN ATOMIC BOMB.
THE BRIEFCASE IS HANDED GINGERLY TO YOUSEF.
KLIK
IN IT IS ENOUGH PLUTONIUM FOR A BOMB WHICH COULD LEVEL A GOOD-SIZED SECTION OF A CITY...
...THIS CITY.

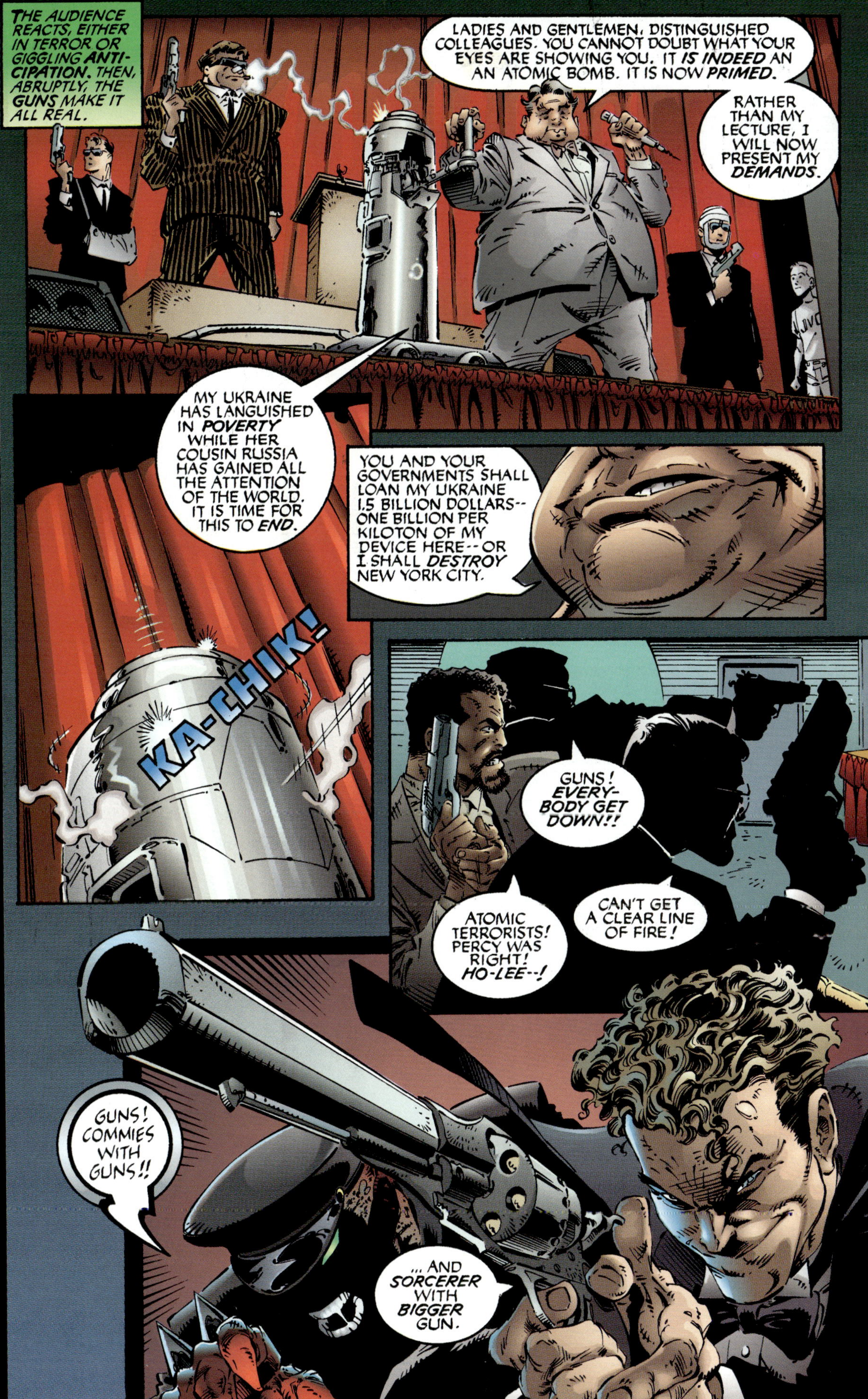

THE AUDIENCE REACTS, EITHER IN TERROR OR GIGGLING ANTICIPATION. THEN, ABRUPTLY, THE GUNS MAKE IT ALL REAL.
LADIES AND GENTLEMEN, DISTINGUISHED COLLEAGUES. YOU CANNOT DOUBT WHAT YOUR EYES ARE SHOWING YOU. IT IS INDEED AN AN ATOMIC BOMB. IT IS NOW PRIMED.
RATHER THAN MY LECTURE, I WILL NOW PRESENT MY DEMANDS.
MY UKRAINE HAS LANGUISHED IN POVERTY WHILE HER COUSIN RUSSIA HAS GAINED ALL THE ATTENTION OF THE WORLD. IT IS TIME FOR THIS TO END.
YOU AND YOUR GOVERNMENTS SHALL LOAN MY UKRAINE 1.5 BILLION DOLLARS-- ONE BILLION PER KILOTON OF MY DEVICE HERE-- OR I SHALL DESTROY NEW YORK CITY.
KA-CHIK!
GUNS! EVERY- BODY GET DOWN!!
ATOMIC TERRORISTS! PERCY WAS RIGHT! HO-LEE--!
CAN'T GET A CLEAR LINE OF FIRE!
GUNS! COMMIES WITH GUNS!!
...AND SORCERER WITH BIGGER GUN.

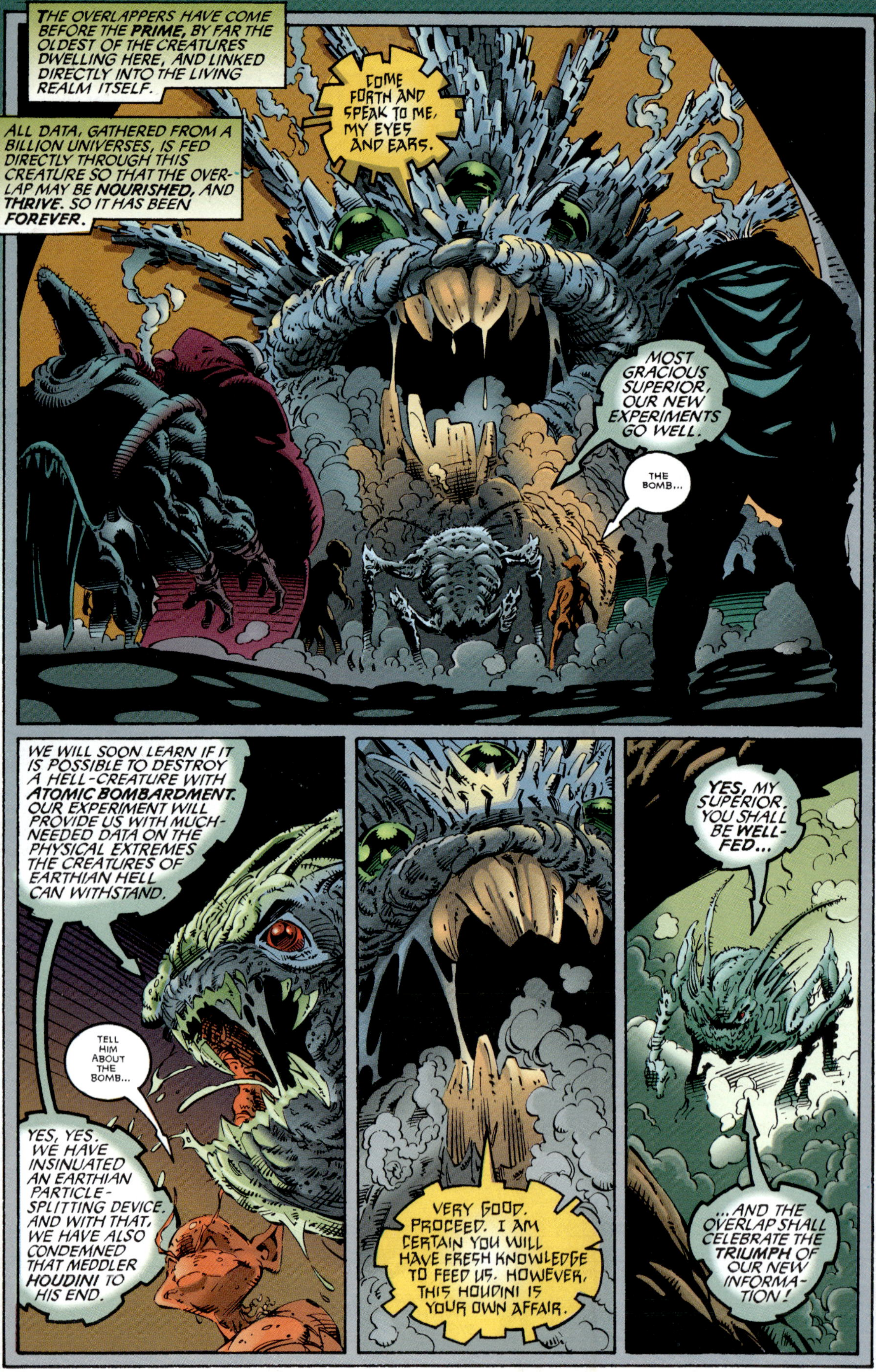

THE OVERLAPPERS HAVE COME BEFORE THE PRIME, BY FAR THE OLDEST OF THE CREATURES DWELLING HERE, AND LINKED DIRECTLY INTO THE LIVING REALM ITSELF.
ALL DATA, GATHERED FROM A BILLION UNIVERSES, IS FED DIRECTLY THROUGH THIS CREATURE SO THAT THE OVERLAP MAY BE NOURISHED, AND THRIVE. SO IT HAS BEEN FOREVER.
COME FORTH AND SPEAK TO ME, MY EYES AND EARS.
MOST GRACIOUS SUPERIOR, OUR NEW EXPERIMENTS GO WELL.
THE BOMB...

WE WILL SOON LEARN IF IT IS POSSIBLE TO DESTROY A HELL-CREATURE WITH ATOMIC BOMBARDMENT. OUR EXPERIMENT WILL PROVIDE US WITH MUCH-NEEDED DATA ON THE PHYSICAL EXTREMES THE CREATURES OF EARTHIAN HELL CAN WITHSTAND.
TELL HIM ABOUT THE BOMB...
YES, YES. WE HAVE INSINUATED AN EARTHIAN PARTICLE-SPLITTING DEVICE. AND WITH THAT, WE HAVE ALSO CONDEMNED THAT MEDDLER HOUDINI TO HIS END.

VERY GOOD. PROCEED. I AM CERTAIN YOU WILL HAVE FRESH KNOWLEDGE TO FEED US. HOWEVER, THIS HOUDINI IS YOUR OWN AFFAIR.

YES, MY SUPERIOR, YOU SHALL BE WELL-FED...
...AND THE OVERLAP SHALL CELEBRATE THE TRIUMPH OF OUR NEW INFORMATION!

WHILE, ON EARTH, THE TEST CONTINUES...
PLEASE, EVERYONE TO REMAIN CALM. YOUR GUNS WILL NOT STOP US.
!!!
KOOM
ALWAYS THE PERFORMER, HOUDINI STARTS THE SHOW WITH A SHOT INTO THE AIR.
FRAYED NERVES SNAP. INSTINCT DIRECTS SHOTS AT THE ONLY FAMILIAR TARGET: SPECIAL AGENT FITZGERALD.
BLAM
JEE-ZUS!
NOOO!

THE EXITS ARE FEW AND FAR BETWEEN. CHAOS ENSUES.

FOOLS. IT WOULD HAVE BEEN SO SIMPLE.
BAM
CHUK
KLIK

YOU IDIOTS! ENOUGH!! I HAVE STARTED THE TIMER!
LEGGO, IGOR!
ARMED
BIDEEP
BIDEEP
BIDEEP
TO NATION
IF YOU DO NOT END THIS MADNESS, THE BOMB WILL END IT FOR YOU.

THANK YOU. I RETURN YOUR LIVES TO YOU FOR NOW.
SKOIP!
JVC

ARMED
BIDEEP
BIDEEP
BIDEEP'O NAT'
BIDEEP

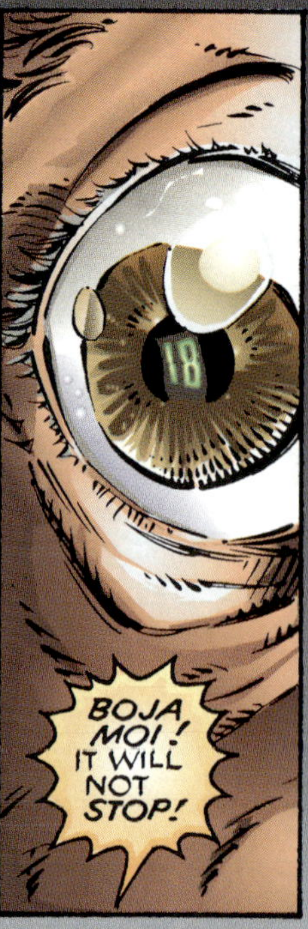

BOJA MOI! IT WILL NOT STOP!

15
I'VE DONE MY BIT. THAT'S MY CUE TO CHECK OUT OF HERE.
AIIIIIIII!
S-KOIP!
THOSE SCHMUCKS HAVE SHUT ME OUT! IT'S TIME I PAID THEM A PIECE OF MY MIND.
CONCENTRATE...
...JUST ANOTHER TRAP...
...GOT MY PATHWAY...
...VISUALIZE...
01
THIS IS OUR MOMENT! TO THINK WE FEARED HOUDINI'S REVOLUTIONARY TALK. I SALUTE YOU, %^9.
I AM GOOD...

FOCUS!!!
HURTS!
TRANSMIT THE BLAST...
...CHANNEL...
...THE BLAST...
REALITY SHATTERS LIKE CANDIED GLASS. THE PART OF OUR UNIVERSE CONTAINING THE BOMB IS TRAPPED BY THE SORCERER, AND SHUNTED INTO ANOTHER PLACE.
THE INSTANT OF THE ATOM'S SPLIT-- THE TIME WHEN FIERCE ENERGIES ARE RELEASED-- NEVER EVEN HAPPENS ON OUR WORLD.
SPAWN CARRIES ON, UNAWARE OF THE PACKAGED MOMENT BEYOND HIM, VENTING HIS RAGE ON TERRY'S ATTACKER.
AS NATURE ABHORS A VACUUM, SO TOO DOES REALITY, ONLY MORE SO. THE STAGE AND OTHER PARTS OF OUR WORLD ARE RENT VIOLENTLY FROM THIS PLANE, FOLLOWING IN THE WAKE OF THE TRANSPORTED BLAST.
MAGICIANS' CLUB STORAGE
COMPRESSED INTO A BEAM OF POWER, THE REALITY ENVELOPE IS SHOVED THROUGH THE MAIL SLOT OF AN UNSUSPECTING ADDRESSEE. BY REFLEX, HOUDINI USES THE MEMORY OF HIS TRUNK AS A FOCUS-- AND SENDS THE TIGHT PARTICULATE STREAM WHERE IT WILL DO THE MOST GOOD.

COLUMBIA UNIVERSITY'S LECTURE HALL IS BUZZING WITH AMAZED SCIENTISTS. THERE WAS LESS THAN A SECOND OF LIGHT-- BUT THAT WAS ENOUGH TO INSPIRE IDLE SPECULATION FOR YEARS TO COME.
FRIED. DAMN. I HAD SO MUCH TO LEARN FROM YOU HOUDINI-- IF YOU REALLY WERE HOUDINI.
A FLASH...
AND THEN...
IT VANISHED...
OR SOMETHING...
DID YOU HEAR SOMETHING?
EH-- IT WAS JUST THE ICE MACHINE DOWN THE HALL.
H. GEIGER 1882-1945
MOMENTS AGO, THESE GEIGER COUNTERS WERE SET OFF THE SCALE BY RADIATION FROM VOLOKHOV'S BOMB.
SO THOROUGH WAS HOUDINI'S MAGIC THAT, FOR A MOMENT, EVEN NORMAL BACKGROUND LEVELS WERE FLAT.

...APPEARS TO BE AN ATTEMPTED NUCLEAR TERRORIST ACTION AT COLUMBIA UNIVERSITY. WHAT YOU ARE SEEING IS AMATEUR VIDEO, SHOWING WHAT WE BELIEVE TO BE TWO OF THE TERRORISTS. POLICE WILL SAY ONLY THAT ONE IS AN AMERICAN, THE OTHER A UKRANIAN NATIONAL, AND THAT THERE WAS SOME SORT OF BOMB THREAT.
WITNESSES CLAIM THAT THOUGH IT SEEMED THERE WAS AN EXPLOSION, THE EVIDENCE IS IN DISPUTE. HOWEVER, THE PRESENCE OF AN ARMED ATOMIC BOMB HAS BEEN CORROBORATED BY ANY NUMBER OF EXPERT WITNESSES.
FIRE CREWS ARE LOOKING FOR ANY POSSIBLE CONNECTION BETWEEN THESE REPORTS AND A BLACKENED PART OF THE HALL WHERE THE STAGE HAD BEEN.
THE ALLEGED THREAT WAS APPARENTLY AVERTED BY A SUSPECTED *YOUNGBLOOD*, THOUGHT TO HAVE BEEN "*FRIED TO A CRISP*" BY SOME UNKNOWN FORCE AT THE SCENE.
THE GOVERNMENT HAS DENIED BOTH THE REPORT OF THE NUCLEAR THREAT AND SUPPOSED EXPLOSION, AND OF ANY YOUNGBLOOD ACTIVITY IN NEW YORK CITY AT THAT TIME. COULD THIS HAVE BEEN A ROGUE 'BLOOD, CONNECTED TO SOME PREVIOUSLY UNKNOWN ORGANIZATION?
CERTAINLY SOMEONE OR SOME*THING* WAS RECORDED LEAVING THE SCENE. HERE WITH AN ANALYSIS...

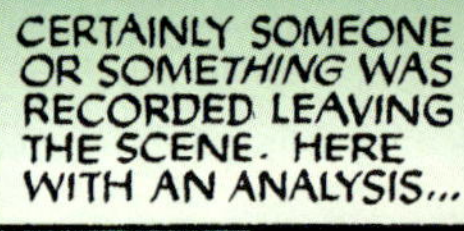

ELSEWHERE ON THE COLUMBIA CAMPUS...
SEEMS HOUDINI LEFT THE CAR INVISIBLE. THAT MAKES IT UP TO ME TO FIND IT.
JUST CONCENTRATE... USE THE COSTUME TO REARRANGE THE PHOTONS... MAKE THE CAR REAPPEAR...
PERFECT. I GUESS I MIGHT BETTER AT MAGIC THAN I THOUGHT.
SORRY ABOUT THE MYSTERY HERE, TERRY, BUT I CAN'T HAVE YOU KNOW ABOUT ME JUST YET.
DAMMIT! HOUDINI HAD THE KEYS!
FINE. I'LL JUST MANIFEST THEM.
EASY!
tssing
WHAT THE--
POOT
BY CREATING THE KEY, SPAWN PASSED HOUDINI'S TEST.
THE CAR'S PURPOSE THUS FULFILLED, IT DEFAULTS BACK TO THE OVERLAP.

BACK IN THE BOWERY, LIFE HAS RETURNED TO NORMAL IN THE HOURS AFTER THE LECTURE..
THE POLICE, LEFT WITH NO EVIDENCE OF A CRIME, HAVE DROPPED ALL CHARGES AGAINST PORSCHE MacNEIL.
I SHOULDA GOT SOME FOOD FROM MOM, TOO. I'M STARVED.
HEY... SOMEONE'S BEEN IN HERE. I--
THOUGH LOUD, THE BLAST WAS HARMLESS. CONFETTI FALLS, A PAPER RAIN CARRYING A NOTE WITH IT.
DON'T EVER MESS WITH ME OR MY ALLEY AGAIN, OR THE NEXT ONE TAKES OUT YOU AND THE WHOLE BUILDING WITH IT.
— SPAWN

THE OVERLAP. TIMELESS AND INFINITE. NOW, ALSO, AT THIS STUDY GROUP'S FORUM, A SCENE OF ATOMIC DECIMATION.
THE EXPERIMENT HAS BLOWN UP IN THEIR FACES.

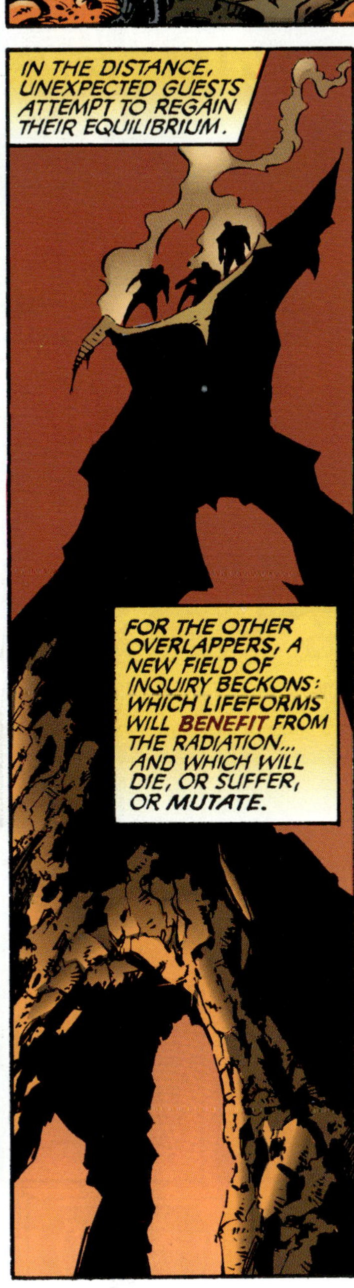

IN THE DISTANCE, UNEXPECTED GUESTS ATTEMPT TO REGAIN THEIR EQUILIBRIUM.
FOR THE OTHER OVERLAPPERS, A NEW FIELD OF INQUIRY BECKONS: WHICH LIFEFORMS WILL BENEFIT FROM THE RADIATION... AND WHICH WILL DIE, OR SUFFER, OR MUTATE.

FOR SOME, THE SUFFERING IS OBVIOUS.
GREGOR... HAVE WE DIED?
WHERE ARE WE? HOW LONG MUST WE STAY HERE?
IS THIS THE AFTERLIFE?
NOT AT ALL, EARTHIAN SCUM! NOW THAT YOUR ENERGY HAS BEEN DAMPENED, YOU HAVE MUCH TO ANSWER FOR, AND EVEN MORE TO CLEAN!
IT WILL BE INTERESTING TO SEE HOW YOUR KIND FARE AGAINST RADIATION BURNS, LITTLE HUMANS. WE HAVE FOREVER TO LEARN!
Raaaht-- CLEAN! CLEAN!
FOREVER! --Raaahtt-- FOREVER!

AGAIN, 1916, ON A STAGE IN LOS ANGELES...
HE HASN'T GOT OUT YET! HARRY SAID RAISE IT AFTER FIVE MINUTES!
THE HUSHED AUDIENCE IS TERRIFIED. NO NORMAL HUMAN BEING COULD HAVE SURVIVED THIS LONG-- FIVE MINUTES!-- WITHOUT AIR.
THE TRUNK IS LOWERED TO THE STAGE.
INTENSITY BUILDS. THE GENTEEL CROWD WAITS BREATHLESSLY. WILL THEY SEE DEATH FIRSTHAND?
ONCE MORE, HARRY HOUDINI HAS MYSTIFIED THEM.
THANK YOU! YOU'RE TOO KIND!
A COUPLE MORE MANACLES AND I WOULDN'T'VE HAD THE SECONDS TO SLIP AWAY AND BACK!
Hm... PERHAPS I CAN WORK THAT "DIVERTED EXPLOSION" GIMMICK INTO MY SHOW.
OF COURSE, %^2 MIGHT HAVE SOMETHING TO SAY AGAINST THAT.
LUCKY FOR HIM, I'LL HAVE TO SAVE THAT ENCORE FOR ANOTHER DAY.
Ahhh... MY PUBLIC. I RETURN FOR YOU YET AGAIN!
WHERE'S HIS CAPE?
THE END

"REFLECTIONS" PART ONE

Grant Morrison – *story*
Greg Capullo – *pencils*
Dan Panosian, Art Thibert – *inks*
Tom Orzechowski – *letters & editor*
Steve Oliff and Olyoptics – *colour*

"REFLECTIONS" PART TWO

Grant Morrison – *story*
Greg Capullo – *pencils*
Mark Pennington – *inks*
Tom Orzechowski – *copy editor & letters*
Steve Oliff and Olyoptics – *colour*

"REFLECTIONS" PART THREE

Grant Morrison – *story*
Greg Capullo – *pencils*
Dan Panosian, Art Thibert – *inks*
Tom Orzechowski – *letters & editor*
Steve Oliff and Olyoptics – *colour*

"SHOWTIME" PART ONE

Tom Orzechowski, Andrew Grossberg – *story*
Greg Capullo – *pencils*
Mark Pennington – *inks*
Tom Orzechowski – *copy editor & letterer*
Steve Oliff and Olyoptics – *colour*

"SHOWTIME" PART TWO

Tom Orzechowski, Andrew Grossberg – *story*
Greg Capullo – *pencils*
Todd McFarlane, Mark Pennington – *inks*
Tom Orzechowski – *copy editor & letterer*
Steve Oliff and Olyoptics – *colour*